THE AFRICAN MASK

THE AFRICAN MASK

by Janet E. Rupert

HOUGHTON MIFFLIN

Boston • Atlanta • Dallas • Geneva, Illinois • Palo Alto • Princeton

Thanks to the many people who have helped to create
this book. Special thanks to John Rupert,
Mary Anne Gladys, Dr. Lewis Ulman,
Dr. Janet Hickman, Dr. Ojo Arewa, and Kemi Adejare.

Clarion Books
a Houghton Mifflin Company imprint
215 Park Avenue South, New York, NY 10003
Copyright © 1994 by Janet E. Rupert

The text was set in 12/15-point Sabon.

For information about this and other Houghton Mifflin trade and reference
books and multimedia products, visit The Bookstore at Houghton Mifflin
on the World Wide Web at (http://www.hmco.com/trade/).

Printed in the USA

Library of Congress Cataloging-in-Publication Data

Rupert, Janet E.
The African mask / by Janet E. Rupert.
p.   cm.
Summary: Twelve-year-old Layo, a Yoruba girl living in the area
of eleventh-century Africa which is now Nigeria, attempts to reject the man
who has been chosen to be her husband.
ISBN 0-395-67295-3
[1. Yoruba (African people)—Fiction. 2. Nigeria—Fiction.]
I. Title.
PZ7.R8884Af   1994
[Fic]—dc20   93-7726
CIP
AC

56789-B-04 03 02 01 00

For Ben and Eric

▲ ▲ ▲

In memory of Paul Douglas Nelson

FOREWORD

Nine hundred years ago, a dozen villages of the Yoruba people, who lived in the section of Africa now known as Nigeria, came together. They were led by a divine king to carve the city-state of Ife out of the forest. In the cooperative atmosphere of the city, the arts thrived. The Yoruba became well known for wood carvings, terra-cottas, and the finest bronzes cast anywhere in the world.

GUIDE TO PRONUNCIATION

Name		Identity
Abiri	ah-BEE-ree	Layo's village
Ajayi	ah-JAH-yee	a funeral mask is being made for his mother in Ife
Akinlabi	ah-KEEN-lah-bee	Layo's father
Aina	ah-ee-NAH	Bisi's mama
Biodun	bee-oh-DOON	Layo's brother
Bisi	BEE-see	Layo's half brother
Dada	DAH-dah	a young man in Ife
Dunsimi	doon-SEE-mee	a young man in Abiri
Ebun	eh-BOON	a girl in Ife
Ekundayo	eh-KOON-dah-yoh	Yetunde's grandfather

Name		Identity
Esu	EH-shoo	a divinity
Femi	FEH-mee	Layo's brother
Fourmilayo	FOR-mee-LAH-yoh	Olade and Tola's mama, Layo's grandmother
iba	EE-bah	malarial fever
Ife	EE-feh	the holy city
Kemi	KEM-ee	a girl in Abiri
Kosoko	koh-SOH-koh	a boy in Ife
Layo	LAH-yoh	village girl who travels to Ife
Obalara	aw-bah-LAR-ah	Obalufon's son
Obalufon	aw-bah-LU-fon	a bronze caster in Ife, the father of Obalara
Obatala	aw-bah-TAL-ah	a divinity
Oduduwa	oh-DOO-doo-wah	a divinity
Ogbon Oya	AWG-bohn AW-yah	a ward (neighborhood)
Ogboni	awg-BOH-nee	a governing body
Ogun	oh-GOON	a divinity
Ogunkeye	oh-GOON-keh-yeh	Olade's son

Name		Identity
Ogunsanwo	oh-GOON-shahn-woh	Layo's family compound in Ife
Ojo	OH-joh	Layo's youngest brother
Olade	oh-LAH-deh	Layo's uncle, Ogunkeye's papa
Olokun	oh-loh-KOON	where life began, just outside of Ife
Tola	TOH-lah	Layo's mother
Toyin	TOY-een	Layo's cousin in Ife
Wale	WAH-leh	Layo's brother
Winsemi	win-SEH-mee	Layo's compound
Yetunde	yeh-TOON-deh	Layo's cousin in Abiri

THE AFRICAN MASK

Chapter 1

LAYO WOKE WITH A START. She had been dreaming. In her dream there had been drumming and dancing of the kind before one tells a story. She did not remember what had been happening in her dream. She only remembered that there was something she must do now.

Before the first glimmer of light filled the sky above her village of Abiri, twelve-year-old Layo put on her faded blue work wrapper and crept from her mother's room in the compound. Yes, there was something she *must* do, secretly. Already, aunts, uncles, and cousins were awakening to prepare for the day's work, so she had to move quickly. Ignoring the cool air, she ran to a grove outside the compound where she had prepared and hidden her materials on previous mornings.

Layo was building a clay pot. She pulled the pot base she had made the morning before from under a fallen tree trunk and felt its smooth and perfect lines. Good, it was dry enough to work on.

1

As the sky lightened, the tall, thin girl found her jar of clay, clay she had carefully mixed with just the right amount of broken potsherds on other dark mornings. On a large, smooth rock she rolled out handfuls of the stuff into long snakes. Layo quickly coiled the clay snakes onto the rim of the pot base. Walking around and around her work, she used a wet leaf to seal the coils, and then smoothed them with a bark scraper.

Layo stood back and saw that in her first try ever, she had made as good a cooking pot as she had seen. Layo was proud, but puzzled.

With much practice, and years after her marriage, a woman might be able to make beautiful pots. Yet here was one now. Why?

Layo had been almost certain that she could do it. She had seen the image of this pot in her mind. She had felt it form in her hands before she touched the clay. And she had had to give it form, just to know that she could. But where did this ability come from that should have taken years of practice? Layo didn't know, and she was a little scared.

She longed to show this pot to her grandmother, who was a master of working clay. But even if Grandmother were here in the village, Layo couldn't do that. Adults only wanted her to pound potsherds and maybe build a coarse child's pot someday.

Also, Bisi's mama, her mother's co-wife, might dislike her if she knew. Bisi's mama had been making

2

pots for the three years she had been in the compound, ever since she had become Layo's father's second wife. The woman just couldn't get the coils on smooth and straight. Sometimes Bisi's mama would pick up a pot she had been working on and just toss it to the ground, smashing it. *Well,* Layo thought, *Bisi's mama must not know.*

Layo smiled. The pot wasn't quite finished after all. She picked up a sharp stick and marked the rim of her pot with Bisi's mama's mark. The pot would be a secret gift to her, the youngest wife of the compound. Layo looked for spying brothers or cousins, then hid her supplies again under the rotten log in the grove.

She passed the painted shrine where almost life-size statues stood. The graceful terra-cotta figures had been made by her own grandmother for use in worship. Layo did not go into the sacred area.

She snuck the pot to the potter's area of her compound and set it out to dry among the women's pots.

Her father, Akinlabi, was just leaving his room, ready to work. She bowed as she greeted him.

He said in the Yoruba language, "Good morning, Dark as the Forest. You are late this morning."

"Yes, Papa. I am sorry. It won't happen again."

"All right. Remember to work hard and please your mother."

"Yes, Papa." She bowed again before going to greet her mother.

3

As she bowed to her mother, the woman said, "Layo, you have lingered too long in the forest these past few mornings."

Layo was glad her clay pot was done. People were beginning to notice her absence. "I'm sorry, Mama. I'll be faster."

Then Mama repeated Layo's praise song to her, just as she did every morning:

Winsemi, hunters,
Owners of vision to see in the thick forest,
Providers of food for a whole village in one day,
Layo, daughter of Akinlabi,
Beautiful daughter, she who has skin as dark as the
*   forest.*

Layo smiled. This was who she was, and it was wonderful. No one else's song was the same. Winsemi was the name of her compound, and the part about hunting and food was the praise poem that belonged to the compound. Akinlabi was Papa's name. And the words about skin were her very own. She had beautiful, remarkably black skin.

She was in a good mood when she went to do her chores.

▲▲▲

Yetunde, short and brown and Layo's best friend, joined her. "Layo, where have you been?"

She laughed. "I went to relieve myself in the

4

forest, and a spirit tried to lure me away. It took all my strength to escape."

"Don't joke about such things," Yetunde said solemnly.

"You are right."

Layo lifted a large jar to her head and walked toward the village spring. "Have you gotten water yet?" she called over her shoulder.

"Yes, long ago."

"Well, come along and help me lift this when it's full."

They walked the narrow street between the high mud walls of the village compounds. In the center of Abiri near the chief's compound was an open market area and the spring. Layo met some of the other girls of the village filling their water jars.

"Layo, I saw Dunsimi eyeing you the other day," said Kemi from the chief's compound. "How would you like that, to be the wife of Dunsimi?"

Layo answered, "Dunsimi is round like a cooking pot."

Everyone but Yetunde giggled. She said, "I will marry whomever my parents choose for me. That way, they will continue to look after my interests. Besides, to be the wife of Dunsimi would not be bad. One would be the first wife of the oldest son in the compound."

"Yes, I guess one could get over that roundness," said Layo, and everyone laughed.

When her turn came, Layo dipped her jar into

the depression at the spring and allowed it to fill with cold, clear water. Yetunde helped her lift the heavy jar to her head, and Layo walked to her compound.

There, the white, chalk-covered mud walls and the thatched roof stood out against the green forest and hard-packed, reddish dirt courtyard. There was a room for each adult, connected side by side in a U-shape. The doors all opened onto a roofed veranda that lined the mostly enclosed courtyard.

Nearly a hundred people prepared for the activities of the day in Winsemi compound. Father, uncles, brothers, and boy cousins, dressed in leather, joked and laughed as they sharpened knives and bundled arrows. The *harmattan,* the dry season with its cool night air and hot dry days, was here. Now was the time for hunting in the forest around their village.

The mothers and daughters, all dressed in wrappers of various shades of blue, also happily did their morning chores. A couple of women boiled yams for breakfast on the long veranda, while girls swept their parents' rooms and the verandas off them.

Layo gave her mother the jar of water and grabbed a broom to do her sweeping. Just then she spotted a goat in Bisi's mama's room across the compound. "Hey!" she yelled and ran across the compound waving the broom about. "Get out of there!" Bisi's mama was standing on her veranda with her back to her door. She looked up with astonishment at the sight of Layo running at her with the broom. Just then the goat ran out past her.

Breathless, Layo told Bisi's mama, "It was eating your mat, Mama." All children called anyone who was older either Mama or Papa or, if the person was not old enough to have children, Elder.

"Thank you, Layo," Bisi's mama said. "Those goats are always into everything."

"Mother of Bisi," one of the men called, "bring me my knife from my room."

Bisi's mama closed her door and, with her little boy Bisi bundled on her back, stepped off to do the chore.

In her own mother's room, Layo's mind wandered with the swish, swish of the broom. *Oh, I'm glad I am not yet a new wife of a compound,* she thought. To be a junior to all the adults already there! Now was the time to think about it though. Soon her parents would choose someone for her, and she would be betrothed. At least marriage was still years off.

The main problem was the young men who were available in Abiri. No, the problem wasn't really the young men either. It was the women. None of the women in the men's compounds were potters, and wives took up the craft or trade of the women already there. How would she bear it? To have no clay and to be a junior to all. Layo remembered that Bisi's mama had cried the day she arrived in the compound.

Layo usually ate with girls her own age, her age mates. But today, she took care to sit close to Bisi's mama after they received bowls of hot yams with red palm oil. The air was quickly warming so they sat in the shade of the veranda.

"How do you stand it, Mama?" Layo asked as she ate.

"Stand what?"

"What did the women of your compound do?" Bisi's mama was from another village, and Layo had never visited it.

"They dyed cloth," she said absentmindedly. The woman had mashed some yam for her son, Bisi, and was taking him off her back and out of the cloth she used to carry him in.

"Well, don't you miss that?"

"Not really, everything was always stained blue with indigo. I never saw my mothers without blue hands. Clay dries out the skin, but at least you can wash it off."

"Oh." Layo was silent. So maybe Bisi's mama wasn't so unhappy after all.

"You are full of questions today. Is there anything else?" the woman asked, as she daintily scooped some yam into Bisi's wide-open mouth.

"No, well, yes." Layo blurted out, "Don't you hate it?"

"Hate what?" Bisi's mama asked with curiosity.

"Being a young wife in the compound."

Perhaps that was a question she hadn't expected. The woman's face changed. Quickly it flashed with expression and then the expression was gone—hidden. She said carefully, "It is best to accept one's lot cheerfully. And because I'm cheerful, slowly I am gaining respect."

But Layo was shocked. The woman's words didn't match her expression. Bisi's mama lied. The expression had been anger.

Layo didn't know what to think. Maybe, in a way, Bisi's mama didn't lie. She went about her work cheerfully and, slowly, she was gaining respect. But Layo wanted to know how Bisi's mama felt, and she had told her only what she did. Maybe she had just asked the question wrong.

"Thank you for answering my questions, Mother of Bisi. I should join the girls of my age."

"Layo," the woman said as she hugged Bisi, "I have a child; that is the most important thing."

▲▲▲

After a morning of hauling new clay from the clay pit to the compound, the women enjoyed a long lunch. The children sang while one of the little boys tried to drum. It was too hot to work at midday.

Bisi's mama chatted politely with the father of Ekundayo, an old, old man. His status had been *eru*. After being captured in battle with his non-

Yoruba village, he had been given as a war prize to the head of the compound. For many years, his only right had been the right to live.

Everyone knew Ekundayo's papa had been *eru*—he spoke with accented tones—but no one dared speak of it openly. To do so would anger the head of the compound because Ekundayo's papa had been so faithful. The man had worked hard and proved himself trustworthy, and eventually had become part of the family.

Now Ekundayo's papa was too old to go hunting or farm his land as he used to. He stayed here with his daughter and grandchildren. One of his grandchildren was Yetunde, Layo's friend and cousin.

Bisi's mama finished her conversation, bowed, and wandered off. Layo's mother called, "Come, girls, we must prepare the clay."

Under the shade of a big tree at the edge of the compound, Layo and her cousins went back to work. Some stood and pounded old broken pots into little potsherds with a big mortar and pestle. Some kneaded clay with water to the right consistency. Some took care of the younger children. The women made pots from the prepared materials.

The pot Layo had made sat undisturbed in a large assortment of pots drying in the sun. She hoped it didn't crack when it was fired. She wondered if Bisi's mama would notice it.

"Soon we'll have enough pots to fire," Layo said when she took some clay to her mother. "Then we can go to market and sell them."

Layo's mama set aside a finished pot to dry in the sun on the hard-packed courtyard. "Don't you worry about selling them," her mother said, smiling. "Worry about making yourself pretty for the young men at market."

Layo was surprised. Her mother had never spoken of this before. "Yes, Mama." Layo hesitated. "Mama?"

"Yes, Layo."

"I really like to work clay."

"I know, dear." She picked up a lump of clay. "I do, too. It brings me money."

"Mama?"

"Hmm?"

Layo forced the words out. What if her mother said no? "When you choose a husband for me, could you choose one with potters in the compound?"

Mama sighed and put the clay down. "You know, Layo, a woman doesn't always have to take up the trade of the compound."

"She doesn't?"

"No. I remember before you were born, Titilayo's husband paid to have her learn to weave in the chief's compound. The woman said she just couldn't pound yams for a living for another day."

"Then I could come back here . . . to learn . . .

11

to learn to make pots, or even make terra-cottas with Grandmother?"

"Perhaps you could," Mama said. "You should speak to her about that. Now return to work. We must have these pots fired by market day, when my mama arrives. One might think with all this talk that you are not serious-minded."

"Oh, I am serious-minded, Mama," Layo called as she ran to work clay. Everything was right with the world, and soon, Grandmother would arrive.

Chapter 2

LATE IN THE AFTERNOON a day later, Layo was helping clean up the site where the pots had been fired. Gray ashes and black soot covered the reddish soil in a cleared area outside the compound. She was scooping up the ashes with the soap maker when she heard the poetry of the village praise-singer.

"My old mama must be here!" Layo cried out. She rushed to wash her hands and quickly ran a clean rag over them to dry.

Her tall, thin grandmother stepped lithely into the compound with her wares carefully balanced on her head. The woman was called Olade's mama after her son in the city of Ife. White spirals covered her deep blue wrapper. The praise-singer followed her. Women bowed and men prostrated themselves on the ground before their elder. Layo's father helped the old woman put down the net holding her pots, and then prostrated himself before his mother-in-law. The singer called:

Ogunsanwo, masters of black metal,
One makes the tool that cuts the ground,
Fourmilayo, mother of Tola and Toyin,
Mother of Olade, mother of sons,
She who has grace,
Guests are ashamed to dance in her presence,
Fourmilayo, one who transforms cool mud to life.

Layo's pride grew. This was *her* grandmother. She hoped that one day she would be old and receive such honor and respect.

"Greeting to your home," said Olade's mama to Papa in her Ife accent, as she paid the praise-singer cowries, little shells used as money.

"It will hear your greeting, Mother," replied Papa. "Welcome."

The family gathered around Olade's mama to visit and hear news from the city of Ife, where Layo's mother had grown up. Adults were talking now. With proper respect Layo waited her turn to greet Olade's mama. Oh, but she wanted to run up and tell her grandmother everything. She had made a beautiful cooking pot and it had come through the firing! No, she couldn't say that. The old woman was likely to scold her for doing a grown-up's work.

After a little while Olade's mama said to Layo's mother, "Tola, let's see the children."

"Femi, Wale, Layo, Biodun, Ojo! Come greet your mother." Her mother was their mother as well, following the custom of the people.

Layo and her four brothers prostrated themselves before their grandmother. Starting with the oldest, Olade's mama called them to her and greeted her grandchildren in turn with each child's own praise poem. She also asked the child how he was and if he had been working hard. The woman called first for Femi, then Wale, and then Layo.

To Layo she said:

Winsemi, hunters,
Owners of vision to see in the thick forest,
Providers of food for a whole village in one day,
Layo, daughter of Akinlabi,
Beautiful daughter, she who has skin as dark as the
*   forest.*
One who will be easily betrothed.

Layo smiled at the new words Olade's mama had added.

"Layo, you will soon be a woman. I imagine you are attracting the attention of many young men at market."

"Maybe a little, Mama," Layo said shyly.

"Is there anyone you like or anyone who likes to talk to you?"

"For a while Dunsimi talked to me. His mama talked to my mama about a betrothal. Mama told

15

them the diviner said no. Now Dunsimi talks to Yetunde."

Layo knew the truth. Her mother had never spoken with the diviner. There was something about Dunsimi's family Mama didn't like, and she had used the diviner for an excuse.

"Ah. And have you been working hard?"

"Oh, yes, Mama. I have been helping my mothers very much with the clay. I like it a lot." Layo's large black eyes sparkled. "I made something."

"Yes? Let's see it."

This great woman's interest excited her. Layo ran to her mother's room to get a little child's pot she had made. It was a bank for holding cowries, no bigger than her two fists together, with a narrow neck. Breathless, she handed the sturdy and smoothly finished pot to Olade's mama.

"This is fine work," the woman said, thoughtfully turning it over in her hands. "Tomorrow," she said seriously, "this can share my mat in market."

"Oh, thank you, Mama," Layo cried. "I am honored." The girl bowed to her grandmother again and again, as the old woman called the next child, Biodun.

▲▲▲

On market day, under the fig tree, Olade's mama set out her wares on her mat along with Layo's little bank. All the women were there in the

16

shaded market square. Already a hot breeze dried sweat as it formed. The constant buzzing of insects was a background for the many quiet voices selling and buying and visiting. The market wouldn't become truly lively until the evening, when the men returned from the hunt.

Layo, looking very pretty with her hair in small braids, sat on the edge of a mat. She was dressed in a fine, shiny, deep blue wrapper.

"Layo, stay here to sell my wares," Olade's mama ordered. "I want to look at some of the women's work."

Layo looked at the curious assortment of black, red, and yellow pots spread out. Some were for cooking, others for storage. She was surprised. No one woman made such an assortment. Usually, a potter specialized in and perfected one pot. Well, *none* of them had Olade's mama's mark. She had brought only others' work from Ife.

Of course, it occurred to her, Olade's mama only made terra-cottas on commission, mainly masks. But surely the woman hadn't made this trip just to sell others' work. Layo felt fairly certain she had brought these pots so as not to waste her labor on the trip. So why had she really made the trip? She had come before to make a commissioned object for a priest or a chief, or when Mama had a baby. None of these things was happening now.

Layo watched as her expert grandmother went

from mat to mat and examined the different pots. After a while the old woman stopped at Bisi's mama's mat. Bisi's mama got up awkwardly with the baby on her back and gave a bow, and the two women chatted. Olade's mama singled out and picked up the large cooking pot that Layo had made. Olade's mama said something to Bisi's mama as she turned the pot over in her hands. Bisi's mama laughed a little and shrugged. Olade's mama put the pot down and moved on.

Layo smiled. Bisi's mama must certainly be confused. But at least she will get cowries for her confusion, the girl thought, as one of the women from another compound stopped to bargain for the pot.

▲▲▲

"Layo, tell us a story," said a little girl of Winsemi compound early that evening. The older children were taking turns. During the day one could tell only true stories. Now was the time to talk and tell imaginary stories.

Layo began with a story her mother had told her. "There was once a beautiful maiden who scorned all suitors. This one wasn't handsome enough, she said. That one was boring. Her parents were at their wits' end.

"One day the maiden sat in market selling her mother's weaving, when an extraordinarily handsome man in fine, expensive clothes approached

18

her and bargained for cloth. 'I want to be your wife,' she said.

"'No,' he said.

"'I insist,' she answered.

"'No, you would regret it,' he promised, and walked away.

"The maiden followed him. He left the market square with her traveling closely behind. He exited the gates at the walls of the city and she still pursued. Deep through the dark forest the handsome man walked, and the girl followed. She was far from home when she spied a hut. The handsome man knocked on the door of the hut. An old woman answered. 'Thank you for lending me your *eru*'s arms,' he said. And he took off his arms and gave them to her.

"The handsome man continued on and the maiden followed, full of curiosity. Soon they came to a riverbank where some fishermen were sitting repairing nets.

"'Thank you for lending me your legs,' said the handsome man while he took off his legs and gave them to one of the fishermen.

"'Not at all,' replied the man. 'I certainly didn't miss them while sitting here.'

"The handsome man was just a head and torso now. His expensive clothing flopped about as he hopped on.

"The maiden followed him still, filled with concern.

"Dusk quickly fell. At last, after another long trek through strange forest, the handsome man approached a young man sleeping under a tree.

"'Thank you for lending me your torso,' he said to the young man, who had awakened. The handsome Head took off the torso and gave it back to its rightful owner. The Head's expensive clothes lay on the forest floor, as he had no body on which to place them.

"The Head rolled up to the maiden and smiled at her. 'Come be my wife. I live in the crack of that old tree over there.'

"At that, the maiden was overcome by horror. She ran away as fast as she could, while the Head pursued. Fortunately for the maiden, he could not catch her since he had no arms, torso, or legs, but she was lost and alone in the forest."

There was silence when Layo finished speaking.

"That wasn't scary," Biodun declared loudly. "Let me tell you a scary story."

The other children moaned. Biodun wasn't a good storyteller.

Yetunde crept close to Layo. "That story scares me," she whispered.

Layo answered, "Me, too."

Biodun began loudly, "Tortoise was hungry, and his wife was too. Tortoise said, 'I have an idea,' when he heard rooster crow."

As Biodun became sure of his audience's attention, his voice softened. "Tortoise told rooster and the hens, 'Your owner, the housewife, plans to slay one of you for a dinner tomorrow. I overheard her say . . . uh . . . I overheard her say that she will kill the first one of the chickens that makes a sound.'

"Rooster and the hens bowed their thanks and went quietly to roost.

"Early the next morning, tortoise stole all the chickens eggs, but they didn't make a sound."

"Who didn't make a sound?" asked Ojo, Layo's four-year-old brother.

"The chickens," answered Biodun.

Ojo said, "Oh, I thought maybe you meant the tortoise."

"Well, he didn't make a sound either," said Biodun, getting impatient. "They were afraid, see, to cluck or crow because they thought the house-wife would eat them."

"Who's *they* this time?" continued Ojo. "Was the tortoise afraid? I didn't know a tortoise could cluck or crow."

Layo sighed, exasperated. She knew what happened in the story. The housewife was so angry that the chickens had given no warning when the eggs were stolen, she killed them all. And the tortoise profited from his trick. He and his wife had a feast of eggs.

Layo wandered over to where her elders chatted on the veranda. Olade's mama informed Layo's parents, "My daughter in Ife is ready to have her baby. She won't be working for a while, and I need someone to help in her place. It's the dry season, you know, the best time for working clay. The pots and terra-cottas can't dry in the rainy season, and everyone will be busy at their farms, so I need help now.

"My work is so delicate and secret," continued Olade's mama softly, "that I want someone reliable to help me. I must find someone suitable and willing to go back to Ife with me."

Layo listened intently as she sat on the edge of the veranda. So that's why Olade's mama was here. Oh! If only she could go to Ife! All the art and music and dance, markets every day, hundreds of shrines for the many deities, all the people and excitement, the palace and the divine king!

Layo's father asked, "Do you have anyone in mind?"

"Yes, Bisi's mama. I've always seen her to be hardworking and cheerful. She has been a little slow in perfecting her techniques, but today I saw a pot of hers that looked quite fine. I would have been proud to call it my own."

The adults went on with the discussion, but Layo didn't hear. Bisi's mama was going to Ife because of her fine pot! But it was Layo's fine pot. Because of her gift she wouldn't be going to Ife. It was just too much. She felt tears coming and jumped up to go cry alone.

She stumbled in the darkness of the thick forest canopy to the grove where she had hidden her work. She sat on the rotten log where her pottery supplies were hidden, sobbing until her nose stopped up. *Silly girl,* she told herself, Olade's mama wouldn't take her as her main helper no matter what; she wanted an adult. She wiped her wet face with her hands, then dried her hands on her wrapper.

The sun went down and it was suddenly black. There was a soft rustling in the leaves on the forest floor. A puff of air cooled the wet spots on her dress and chilled her. The rustling came closer and she thought of the forest spirits. Then she was even more chilled. She touched a bracelet that her grandmother had given her. It was full of protective medicine.

"*Mo e ri,* I see you," she heard someone call from the distance. Her age mates were playing the hiding game. She swatted at a termite crawling on her leg. The rustling in the leaves was gone. Must have been a mouse. She realized she had been holding her breath and let it out in relief.

She felt silly. Sitting here weeping and getting spooked by mice wasn't doing her any good. She heard more sounds of the game. Her spirits rose.

In the darkness, Layo crept from the grove toward the center of the village. She felt her way along the street between the high compound walls, toward the sound of play. Then she could just see by the light of a single tiny oil flame glowing from the veranda. She stole through a compound. She

23

had to duck under some men's weaving stretched all the way across the courtyard. On the edge of the compound, the girl froze behind a big, fat oil palm. There was the soft pad, pad of bare feet in the dirt. The other person stopped and listened. Whoever it was must be "it." Layo held her breath so they wouldn't hear her. The person turned to walk away. Layo made her move. She leaped out yelling, "Yaah!"

Yetunde shrieked and jumped straight up into the air.

Layo laughed and laughed until Yetunde told her to shut up. "That's not how you play the game. Just for that, you are 'it.'" Yetunde ran off to hide in the dark.

Layo went to seek.

Chapter 3

"Your parents were talking about you," Yetunde told Layo.

Their bare feet left imprints in the cool dust of the street as they carried water jars to fill at the spring. The first dawn light was just spreading over the sky.

"Were you there? Did you hear? What did they say?" Layo asked eagerly, nearly dropping the big jar balanced on her head.

"No, I wasn't there. Your little brother Biodun heard them last night on the veranda while we were playing."

"Well, what did Biodun say? Is he spreading rumors?" Layo asked with a tone of irritation.

"He said they were talking about finding a suitable husband for you. Your mama from Ife said she knew of a family that she liked. They are healthy, hard-working, debt-free, and somewhat wealthy." Yetunde paused.

"What else? What compound are they from?" She ran over the names of the village compounds in her mind and wondered which it could be.

"That's all. His friends called him away to play."

Layo wailed, "Who is this family?"

"That's an interesting question," Yetunde said as she put down her jar on a mossy rock by the spring in the open area of the market. Kemi and several of her sisters, from the chief's compound, were already there.

"Hey, Layo," called Kemi. "Your little brother says you are getting betrothed soon. It's about time. You're getting up there." Kemi had been betrothed since she was ten.

Layo just smiled and said nothing to Kemi. She turned to Yetunde and said quietly, "I'm going to smack Biodun for not telling me first. Besides, he's just a child. Who knows if it's true?"

Layo steadied herself on the wet, slick rocks around the trickle of welling water and bent to fill her jar with water scooped up in a gourd. As Kemi was walking away with her water jar, Layo heard her say, "Layo's mama . . ."

Layo paused and tried to listen, but missed a few words. She did hear Kemi end with, "No wonder she doesn't have a husband yet." Kemi's sisters laughed.

"Kemi, what did you say about my mama?" Layo called.

Kemi carefully turned to face Layo. "I didn't

say anything about your mama. I said my mama."

Layo stared. She knew that wasn't true. "It's a good thing you weren't talking about my mama, 'cause if you were, I might have an answer . . . about your mama," she said.

A grim light stole over Kemi's face. With a grunt she lowered her water jar to the ground. She strutted toward Layo.

"Good morning, girls," Bisi's mama called from the path. She had a jar on her head, and Bisi was wrapped on her back. "Kemi, is there something wrong? Perhaps you would like help lifting your water jar?"

Kemi hesitated a moment, bowed to her elder and said, "Yes, please."

Bisi's mama put down her own jar and silently helped Kemi, who quickly hurried away after her sisters.

"What was that all about, Layo?" Bisi's mama asked.

"Kemi was talking about my mama and laughing."

"Oh? Which mama?"

"I don't know."

"Well, you know she could have been talking about any of the women of the compound, including me. Thank you for defending my honor."

Bisi's mama let the boy splash in the puddles, while they all filled their jars. The woman looked tired.

27

Layo said, "I could get water for you sometimes, Mama."

"Why, thank you, Layo. That is very kind of you. But this water isn't for me. I'm getting this for Ekundayo's papa." Bisi screamed with delight at his splashing.

"Mama, that is very kind of you."

"Thank you."

Layo left to look for Biodun. Biodun was fortunate. He had already left with their father for the day's hunt.

She was angry when she joined in the day's labor making pots. Sometimes Layo was allowed to help mix the clay, but today she smashed old broken pottery using the mortar and pestle. She lifted the big pestle and dropped it down. Crack! There, that one was for Biodun. Crunch! That one was for Kemi. Soon the broken pot was a fine mass of chips in the mortar. Her anger slipped away as she fell into the rhythm of her favorite work. She smashed pot after pot.

Layo's wrapper loosened. It was so hot she secured it to her waist, leaving her chest exposed. That was all right here in the compound.

This wasn't the first time she had overheard comments about her mama. And it always happened when Olade's mama was visiting. What did it mean? What did they know about Olade's mama or some other woman in the compound that made them laugh? She just didn't know.

She could feel tender spots where the calluses were growing on her hands from the pestle, but she ignored them as her imagination carried her away. She was an old woman making ritual pottery. She called the proper spirit to the pottery and so imbued the object with life. One could then call on the being during prayer. A priest gave her honey, some of which she sacrificed to Iya Mapo, Mother Earth . . . there in a darkened room, dark like the thick forest.

"My, you are a good worker," said Old Mama's voice over her shoulder.

The words brought her back with a jolt. Layo stopped her work and dipped her head in a bow. Having received praise, now seemed a good time to ask a favor. "Thank you, Mama. . . . Mama, I heard you tell my parents you need a helper . . . and you want to take Bisi's mama. . . ."

"Yes, that's true, Layo."

"I was wondering. Could you use another helper? I am willing."

Olade's mama kept a solemn expression. But she didn't say no.

"I am a good worker. I wouldn't be any trouble." Layo's enthusiasm grew. "I could help take care of Bisi. And meet my family in Ife. Oh, please, Mama!"

"Wouldn't you miss your family and friends here?" asked Olade's mama, still solemn.

"Yes, of course, but I would have you and my

aunt and uncles in Ife," Layo said, solemn herself.

"Well, Layo, you have given me something to think about. Have you asked your papa if you can go?"

"No."

"Well, girl, you must ask him. I think that your presence could be helpful, but we will abide by your father's decision."

"I will ask him, Mama," Layo called excitedly, as the woman walked away.

Layo turned again to the mortar and pestle with energy. She pounded pot after pot until her shoulders were aching. Sweat dripped from her face into the mortar and her hands were very sore. All the while, it seemed the day would go on forever. She must talk to Papa. So many questions. She had forgotten to ask about the family with a potential husband for her. But children must wait until evening when the day's work was done to question parents or speak with friends.

At lunch, Layo sat drained of energy. Yetunde brought her a bowl of soup.

"Thank you, Cousin," she said weakly.

"Hey, Layo, you are a hard worker, but we still have the afternoon to go," Yetunde said as she sat next to Layo in the shade of the veranda.

"I'm not working hard to work hard," Layo declared.

"Huh?"

"First I was angry. Kemi and Biodun made me angry. It helps to smash things instead of thinking evil thoughts." Layo lowered her voice to almost a whisper. "I wouldn't want to be a witch and harm them with my thoughts."

Yetunde nodded knowingly.

"Then I was just impatient," Layo continued in a normal voice. "I asked my mama if I could go to Ife with her, and—"

"You did?" Yetunde asked, wide-eyed. "What did she say?"

"I have to ask my papa. She said that I could be a help to her."

"Oh, Layo," Yetunde said excitedly, "I think you are going to get to go." Yetunde hugged Layo, almost spilling her soup.

"Well, maybe. Maybe Papa will say no. But don't be like Biodun. Don't go tell everyone before Papa even hears about it."

"I won't. But Layo, what am I going to do? My best friend is leaving. I will live to hear the stories about Ife that you bring back."

The two girls went back to work. Layo pushed herself to keep up the morning's pace. Her actions cried, *I am a good worker. You can count on me.*

▲▲▲

Late in the afternoon, Layo and the other girls of the compound went for their daily bath in a stream outside the village. They walked a narrow forest path carrying bundles of laundry to do after they bathed.

Layo left her wrapper on a big rock and waded into the cooling water, wearing only her waist beads. The other girls laughed and giggled and told stories, but she quietly sat in the stream and pretended the flowing water was carrying all her tiredness away.

Yetunde sat down next to her. "Layo, I have been thinking all afternoon about your trip to Ife. What if some man there chooses you to be his wife? Then you would come back only for a few years until you marry."

Layo hadn't thought of that. She had been so caught up in the excitement of going to the city and the idea of being with a master potter, Olade's mama.

"I don't know about that," she said slowly. "All girls must leave their father's compound and go where their mothers arrange. But I never thought about leaving Abiri." Layo sat for a minute frowning, with the cold water flowing around her, then said, "I don't know, Yetunde. I just don't know. Maybe I shouldn't go."

"The water that one is destined to drink does not flow past one," Yetunde replied. "Excuse me if that sounded like a proverb. But you know, Layo, whatever is destined to happen, will happen. If you are meant to marry outside of the village, it will happen whether you go to Ife or not."

"You are right." Layo felt much better. There was no choice in her marriage or future, so why worry? The Creator had helped her choose her fate before she was born. Maybe asking to go to Ife was just playing out a part of her story.

She got her soap and finished washing, then began laundering her clothing. Her beliefs helped her to feel peaceful, though she was eager to talk to Papa.

▲▲▲

"Papa," Layo said that night, bowing to her father.

"Yes, Dark as the Forest?" her father said.

"I come to beg a favor," she said, bowing again.

"What is it? Do you want cowries to buy a new wrapper at market?"

"No, Papa, I want . . . I want to help my mama's mama."

"You do help your mama every day."

"Thank you. But I want to help her in Ife." Layo continued quickly, "I could help Bisi's mama with Bisi, too, if she gets to go."

"Well, that's an interesting idea. I think that tomorrow your mother can take you to the diviner. If the diviner says it's a good idea, then you shall go."

"Oh, thank you, Papa, thank you!" Layo bowed and then hugged her father, and her mother, too. "Oh, I hope, I hope I can go," she called as she ran to tell Yetunde, forgetting her other concerns. And in her excitement, she didn't stop to wonder why getting Papa's approval had been so easy.

Chapter 4

LAYO AND MAMA STOPPED by an iron post topped with cast-iron birds. Death would stop to take the rooster sacrificed upon it and leave the diviner's clients alone.

The diviner was also called *babalawo*, the father of the secret.

The diviner's compound had many wooden posts carved in the shapes of men and women that held up the veranda roof. The carvings symbolized the importance of people and the importance of men and women working together. They were a mark of wealth and prestige.

Layo and Mama spied Bisi's mama leaving by the intricately carved door. She handed the *babalawo* a large pot full of cowries, bowed, and turned away. Bisi's mama's mouth was set hard in a straight-across line. Mama greeted Bisi's mama, and her co-wife returned the greeting, then quickly stepped away. Bisi began to cry but his mama ignored him.

"What's wrong with Bisi's mama, Mama?"

34

"She must have had a difficult session."

"Will that happen to us?"

"Perhaps, but by making the proper sacrifice, one can rest easy."

"Bisi's mama must have had to make a *large* sacrifice," said Layo, referring to the large pot of cowries, which would be used by the diviner to purchase an animal to sacrifice, to placate the Creator.

"Yes," her mother agreed as she and Layo bowed before the old diviner, who was dressed in a fine, white shirt and trousers. White was a sacred color. It represented the bloodless sacrifice.

Layo had known this man all her life. Mama greeted him and said, "I wish to talk with the divinity."

He invited them into his room, leaving the door open to allow in light. Even then Layo could just see the objects on the shrine in one corner of the room.

"Please be seated," invited the *babalawo*. Layo and Mama sat on the multicolored mat. Layo could feel her heart thumping while the diviner took his tray and stick, then a jar from the shrine, and placed them next to himself. The diviner sat with his legs stretched out, the carved, round tray between them.

The *babalawo* took the divining chain, which was made of nuts on a string, from the jar. He handed the chain to Mama. She whispered her question to it and gave it back.

He gently tapped on the tray in order, Layo guessed, to attract the attention of the divinity that resided in the shrine to the tray. The man of medicine opened the jar and spread a white powder from it to the center of the tray.

"Ifa, I greet you. Please answer this question quickly." He murmured some words of poetry in which he asked for the blessing of earthly authorities and the blessing of the Creator.

The diviner took up the divining chain and cast it on the ground. Some of the nuts landed rough side up, and some, smooth. With the stick he made one mark in the dust on the tray and cast again. Two marks. Again, two marks, and last cast, one.

He smiled. "Odi Meji," he said. He recited in his soft, old voice:

> Gateman, open the gate wisely.
> Gateman, open the gate wisely.
> Open the gate for money,
> Open the gate for wife.
> Gateman, open the gate wisely.

He paused. "Does this fit your situation?"

Mama shook her head.

The priest continued:

> I arrive well,
> I travel well.

*I am he who usually travels and comes across
fortune.*

"Yes," Mama said.

"This one is simple. Someone in your family
will journey and have great good luck. But it is
linked with the previous verse. This person will
only have good luck if the person recognizes what
to accept and what to reject, like a man guarding a
gate. Now we must ascertain who this verse is
for."

Layo's excitement rose as he handed Mama a
bone and two cowries. Mama cupped one hand in
the other to shield the small items from view. She
brought her hands apart, the bone and cowries
hidden in her closed fists.

"Ifa, you say you see luck in travel. Who is this
for? Is this for my client?" The *babalawo* cast
again and again, making marks in the dust in the
tray. "This second verse is senior. Ifa chooses the
right hand."

Mama opened her right hand. The bone was in it.

"Ifa says no. Is this luck then for this child, my
client's daughter?" he continued.

Layo felt someone was watching her at this
important moment in her life. Was that the presence of the divinity?

The diviner cast again.

"Senior. Ifa chooses the right hand again."

Mama opened her right hand. There lay two

cowries. Layo hadn't noticed that Mama had switched them while the priest was working.

"Ifa says yes. The verse is for her."

He set aside his tools and looked intently at Layo. "I want you to understand what the verses mean."

"Yes, Father?" She lowered her gaze to answer respectfully.

"Many things will happen to you when you journey," he said, his voice thin with age. "Some things will be good and some will be bad. You won't always be able to tell the difference right away. So you must think: 'Is this something that will help me and my family in the long run?' If it is, all you have to do is accept it, and with your good fortune it will be yours. That will be your work, to think like a gateman and know when to open the door. Do you understand?"

"Yes," she said solemnly. Layo did understand, but she felt a burden. Why couldn't she just get good fortune, instead of having to choose the right thing?

Mama was giving the diviner cowries for the sacrifice of red palm oil that he prescribed. The diviner had the palm oil, which he poured on the red clay mound of Esu. "Esu, we beg you; carry this message to the Creator; carry out this child's best fate."

After they left, Layo asked Mama, "Why do I have to make choices? Why can't I just have good fortune?"

"Why, Layo, your fate is better than some. Some people are fortunate only with great sacrifice. Your fate says that your good fortune will come with just a little thought."

"Yes, I guess so." But Layo was worried. What if she chose wrong? Would her good fortune pass her by?

"And you know what this means, don't you?" Mama was smiling.

Slowly, Layo realized what the smile was for and her burden lightened. She grinned. "Yes. I am going to Ife."

▲▲▲

Layo could barely keep from talking all morning while working. Only the fear that her parents would change their minds if she did not behave seriously kept her from it.

She was curious, too. Olade's mama had received a commission for a mask from the *egungun* cult, the ancestor masqueraders. She was working on it inside, in the dimness, in contact with the earth. But Layo dared not look in the door.

Olade's mama was, in a secret way, imbuing the mask with power and life—not a thing a little girl could withstand, nor even a young woman. Only old women were not struck dead by the energy of it.

As she worked for the mothers, Layo had seen her grandmother come outside once. The old woman, in her faded blue work wrapper, had rinsed a wooden cutting tool and a bark scraper in a jar of water, then oiled the cutting tool. Layo had never seen such a tool before and assumed it was special.

Now it was lunchtime, and Layo was chattering. "I hope I get to see the palace."

"Maybe you'll see the *oba*," said Ojo. The *oba* was the king.

"Oh no," she said gently. "The *oba* has so much power, if one saw him, one would die. The *oba* is a divinity."

Ojo's eyes got big. "Don't his wives ever see him?" he asked.

Layo had never pondered that. "Well, I don't know. Maybe they go through ritual or have medicine that lets them withstand his power."

Ojo seemed satisfied with this explanation. He said to his sister, "Tell me a story about Ife."

Layo was delighted. She sat on her parents' bench on the veranda, and all the girls and little boys gathered round. She said hesitantly:

"In the beginning, there was nothing but the sky above and a stormy ocean-covered world below. The Creator, Olodumare, who exists in an invisible, spiritual world, instructed the god Obatala to leave the spirit world and come to the physical world. Olodumare wanted to create life and civilization."

As she searched for words to express the tale,

she remembered how her father had told her the story. Her voice became stronger as many of Papa's words came back to her.

"Obatala came down to the earth on an iron chain, taking with him a snail shell filled with dirt, a five-toed chicken, and a chameleon. The god poured the dirt onto the water and released the chicken. The bird scratched in the dirt and spread it around, creating dry land."

She repeated what her father had said:

"You can see the place at the Olokun grove just outside the city. Then Obatala released the chameleon, which walked on the land to test its firmness, and then he began to create people. But Obatala drank much palm wine. The people he created were extraordinary. Some were blind, some had hunchbacks, some were very short, and some had very white skin. Obatala's wife, Oduduwa, took over the job of creating life. The goddess Oduduwa then became the first ruler of Ife and the mother of all the people," Layo finished solemnly.

Ojo exclaimed and jumped up and down. "Layo is going to where the world began! Layo is going to where the world began!"

"Yes." She smiled. "I am going to the center of the earth."

That night the family relaxed in the compound before retiring. Only familiar rustlings came from the surrounding forest.

Everyone was safely back from the hunt. The goats were tethered and the chickens were caged. The quiet murmur of voices filled the compound. Children played their games in their compounds and throughout the village. Mama and Papa sat on a bench on the veranda in front of Papa's room. A single flame illuminated the night.

"When will we be leaving?" Layo asked her mama and grandmother as they sat on the veranda. Papa talked to Bisi's mama in front of her room. It had been her turn to cook and she was cleaning up after herself. The woman was very quiet.

"In a few days," answered Olade's mama. "I have finished the mask and it's drying. I'll fire it soon; then we can go."

Layo's thoughts ran over the last few days. "I have a question," she said to Olade's mama. Shadows danced around her in the flickering glow.

"That is what the evening is for."

"Biodun has told all the girls he heard you say you found a family you like . . . with a husband for me. Is that true?"

"Yes. That is true."

Layo's heart beat faster. "Oh. Who are they?"

"They are from the Ita Yemoo ward. In Ife. That is why you are going to Ife. So they have a chance to meet you."

42

"Oh, Mama," Layo exclaimed. "I will be away from you!"

She dropped next to her mother and clung to her with her arms around her neck. She missed her mama right then, even though she was still with her. And she felt foolish. She had begged them to let her go when they had planned it all along. With their silence, they had tricked her. She choked back tears.

"Yes, Layo. But you will have our family in Ife." Mama hugged her tightly. "And Layo, there are potters in the man's compound."

Chapter 5

WHEN SHE HEARD TONES drifting in from the forest, the sound sent a shiver of excitement through her. Layo heard the drumming soon after arising, just as she had set out on the street to get water.

She knew the drumming was a message sent from village to farm to village. With the tone drum, a master could imitate the language of the people, repeating popular sayings or well-known poems.

What was this message? The tones repeated many times, then stopped, but not before she got at least some of it. The drums sang, "Fourmilayo, one who transforms cool mud to life." This was a message for Olade's mama.

The message continued, "Death arrives." Layo's stomach churned. More words followed, but she did not know them. Surely Olade's mama would.

She let down her jar as quickly as she could without breaking it. Would she be scolded for putting off her work when a message such as this had arrived? She ran back to the compound.

Olade's mama was talking to Bisi's mama when Layo ran up. "Gather your things. We leave while the shadows are still long," Fourmilayo ordered. Bisi's mama bowed and hurried away.

"Layo, good. You are here. Gather some clothing. Get some pots to sell. Say your good-byes."

"Yes, Mama," Layo said with surprise. "But Mama, what were the last words of the message?"

"One of the *Ogboni* members, the mother of Ajayi, was ill when I left. She has died. I must hurry back to make the mask for her effigy."

"What about the mask you are making here?"

"It can wait," she said, shortly. "The burial can't wait."

"Yes, Mama." Layo understood the urgency now. The burial would take place, at the latest, tomorrow and possibly even today. It depended on how hot it got. The mask would be used along with a wicker body as a substitute for the real body in the lengthy funeral rites.

Layo ran to her mother's room and, in the time that a woman could build a cooking pot, she made a bundle of her clothes, her comb, some beads, and her favorite bark scraper.

Just as she stepped onto the veranda, a man wearing only a loincloth and cutlass ran into the compound. He looked around, breathing very hard, sweat pouring from his body. He spotted Olade's mama, went to her and prostrated himself.

"Wife of Ogunsanwo compound?"

"Yes," Olade's mama answered.

"I am the servant of the mother of Ajayi. I greet you and come to escort you to Ife."

"I accept and return your greeting. We will be ready to go soon."

The man got up, his breathing slower, but red dust now covered the front of his body. Nevertheless, he stood proudly.

"Layo and Yetunde, get some water for the servant of the mother of Ajayi to wash in," Olade's mama ordered.

The girls hurried with their jars to the spring. "Imagine, he ran all the way from Ife this morning. Do you suppose he is *eru*?" Layo asked.

"Maybe, but don't speak so loudly," her friend answered. "Don't be rude. What if he is just a bond servant working to pay the interest on a loan?"

"You are right," Layo said. "I wouldn't want to marry into a family always in debt. They might pawn *me* as a bond servant."

They put down their jars to fill them. "Oh, Layo, you are going away so suddenly," Yetunde cried. "I thought I would have days to talk to you, to say good-bye." She hugged her friend.

"It's not as though I'm leaving forever. I'll be back." There was a catch in her voice. It really was as though she were leaving forever. She would come back only until her wedding.

"I hope this man Mama likes is handsome," Yetunde said.

"Oh, thank you," said Layo, thinking of the round Dunsimi who courted Yetunde. "I will miss you."

Both girls were lost in sobs; the tears welled from their eyes just as the clear water was welling from the earth at the spring.

After a few moments, they wiped their eyes and finished filling the jars. When they returned with the water, the servant was swaggering about the courtyard. "I am a guard at market in Ife. Things go smoothly when I am there," he bragged. The older girls had gathered round, admiring his fine body, but not being so rude as to stare.

"Girls," one of the women called, "it is time to work."

Yetunde and Layo put down their water jars at the edge of the compound, while the other girls reluctantly trudged off to make pottery. The man grabbed a gourd, stripped, and began showering himself with water from the jars.

"Layo, come here, I have something for you," her mother said.

Yetunde and Layo gave each other a last hug and Yetunde joined the others in work.

"Here are some beads. You can give them as a gift to Toyin, your cousin in Ife. She is just your age."

Layo tucked them into her bundle, as well as some pots her mother had made to sell.

"You can keep the money from the sale of the pots to do with as you wish."

"Thank you, Mama."

She sought out Ojo. He squirmed when she hugged him good-bye. "Ojo, tell our brothers good-bye for me. They are all out hunting and I must leave now."

"You are leaving?" he said, looking up at her with large brown eyes. He began to cry.

"Yes, but we are all children of the same mother. We have the most special bond. We will always help each other."

Ojo still cried.

"I'll be back, Ojo."

He stifled his sobs. "Oh," he said.

"Layo!" she heard her mother call. "Have you seen our mama's tools?"

"No, Mama," she answered, surprised.

"They are missing. Help us to look for them around the guest room where Mama stayed."

She walked toward the guest room where a group of women and girls had already gathered to search for the missing tools. Layo looked at the ground on the way to join them and immediately spotted the special wooden cutter at her feet.

"Here is one thing," she called, pointing at the cutter. She was afraid to touch it. A little goat came over and nudged her.

Olade's mama retrieved the cutter. "You have good eyes, appropriate for a daughter of Winsemi compound."

Layo quietly accepted the praise.

"But how do you suppose it got over here?" her grandmother asked.

Layo grabbed the goat pushing at her leg and said, "Need you ask, Mama?"

Old Mama laughed. "Yes, I see what you mean."

A woman handed her a bark scraper. "Thank you," said Olade's mama. "Where did you find it?"

"On the ground by the veranda," said Layo's uncle's third wife.

"How strange. Layo's idea about the goats must be right." Olade's mama called, "Everyone, my tools have been found. Thank you for helping to search for them." She hurried toward her room. "Layo, we must leave soon," she reminded her over her shoulder.

Layo went to say good-bye to her mother.

"Remember what the *babalawo* said. You shall have good fortune. Be a help to your mama and remember to look pretty for the young man."

"Yes, Mama." She bowed deeply; then her mother held her in a last embrace.

The servant, Olade's mama, and Bisi's mama with the child sleeping on her back waited. They all lifted their bundles; the servant carried water for all, and they quickly found the path through the forest north to Ife.

Though it was day, the forest was dark. Layo settled into the pace and breathed a sigh. She looked around her. Layer after layer of trees reached to the sky. It was like being in a vast and living room. The trees were a ceiling, not just blocking, but absorbing the light of the sun.

Because of the darkness, very few plants could grow on the ground. It was easy going along the path, and they were able to make good time.

Layo went first, then Bisi's mama carrying Bisi, then Olade's mama, and finally the servant. That way, the elders could see if anything happened to the young people and protect them. Sometimes there were leopards and big snakes in the trees. The servant had his cutlass.

A few birds called and a band of monkeys chattered in the distance. Mostly, it was quiet except for an occasional snapping of twigs as their bare feet padded across the forest floor.

Layo had walked this way before to farms and other villages, but never as far as Ife.

They walked and walked, keeping track of the distance by landmarks. Here was the chief's land; there was the sacred forest where no hunting was allowed; this path broke off to a village; that rock, finally, marked halfway to Ife. They stopped for a late lunch.

Layo's feet hurt, but she was sent to gather firewood. She was glad to find plenty of fallen wood by the path. This place was just too dark and quiet. The stillness was like trying to be quiet right before one was found in the hiding game. It seemed that at any moment a forest spirit could leap out and take them away, bound magically for all time. She was eager to move on.

Layo set the wood she gathered in a pile by the path. The servant started a fire with flint and began roasting some yams.

Bisi's mama seemed nervous too. She said, "I hope we get there soon."

"Yes," Olade's mama replied. "I want to get to work."

"I just want to be out of this forest."

"Why?"

"I feel so small here. There is so much magic and power."

"This area is not part of the sacred forest, which is full of spirits. But, yes, it is powerful. I feel close to it. The power is for me."

Bisi's mama squinted at Old Mama. Layo knew what she was thinking. If Mama had the power, was she a witch?

Mama guessed what Bisi's mama was thinking too. She said, calmly, her lined face adding to her wisdom, "Perhaps I feel that way because I have worshiped Iya Mapo, Mother Earth, for so long. When I work, I must work in a dark room, my feet touching the earth to get the Mother's power. This place is just an extension of that. The forest is like a great dark room, full of power. Or rather, my room is like a miniature forest. If you decide to specialize in making pottery for sacred rites and worship Iya Mapo, you'll feel the same way. You'll see."

When the yams were done, they ate and moved on. Layo was suddenly happy to be here in the forest after the reminder of Iya Mapo. Potters sacrificed to this divinity, to thank her for her bounty of clay.

"Iya Mapo," Layo sang, taking a step with each word and two more steps before she sang again, "Iya Mapo."

The two women joined in the marching song. Their rising joy and words were a sacrifice to the divinity. When they tired of that song they sang others, giving gifts to the Creator.

Soon they began to meet people who were carrying goods to and from Ife or going out to prepare their farms for the rainy season.

Shafts of light revealed where farm after farm was cut into the protective forest, each with its own hut. There was enough land so that every person who needed it got a parcel. Even the *eru* earned their living by farming their own allotment of land. Some *eru* were able to save enough money from the profits of selling produce to buy their freedom.

▲▲▲

They now walked silently. Layo became alert. She had never before been this close to the city.

They were swarmed by mosquitoes when they

picked a path through a forest swamp. Layo was lucky. Mosquitoes didn't seem to be attracted to her, but she could hear the others slapping away at them.

"We are quite close now," said Mama.

Though insects buzzed, there was still a sense of quietness. Layo felt she should whisper when she talked. She didn't know why. They trudged on through the layers of tree trunks and vines. Suddenly, Layo heard a noise. More insects?

They passed through the trees, and before them was the gate to the great city of Ife. The sound was the activity of the multitude of people living inside.

The gate was freshly constructed with a guardhouse overhead. Men were building a wall of mud on both sides of the gate. Already the sunbaked layers were two times the height of a man and were going higher.

"The *oba* has ordered a wall built around the entire city," said the servant.

"How far is that?" Layo asked.

"Half a morning's walk."

Layo was impressed, having just walked most of the morning and half the afternoon.

"Yes," said Old Mama, "and soon your own village must send materials and men to labor on these walls. This city belongs to all the people, so everyone must help maintain it."

The guard challenged them. Olade's mama paid

a tax with cowrie shells to the *oba* on the goods they planned to sell. Layo wondered how the gate-keeper knew who to let in and who to keep out. But it was daytime—not the time for children to ask questions.

Her question flew from her mind as they entered the holy city of Ife, where life and civilization began.

Chapter 6

LAYO HADN'T NOTICED how cool the forest had been until she walked on the streets of Ife. The light shining through the great slash in the forest dazzled her eyes. After the long walk and now the heat and the light, she was suddenly very tired.

Her exhaustion made the paved streets and whitewashed compounds seem a fantasy. There was compound after compound with carved posts. Here was a mud shrine with incredible faces sculpted into the walls. And there was one white-washed and mural-painted.

Layo had heard stories that there were four hundred one divinities in Ife, each with a shrine. That represented the variety of worship the people could experience in reaching the Creator.

They walked through a maze of compounds. Without a guide, Layo realized, she would have been lost. But there were people everywhere whom she could ask. Men and women and children carried goods to the evening market, and others lined the streets with little stands where they made and sold food.

There were all sorts of people here. Some looked poor with worn, stained clothing; some looked rich with fine fabrics. Well-dressed servants carried long trains of fabric trailing behind their masters. Layo knew some she saw must be either bond servants or *eru,* but she couldn't tell by looking. Sometimes, even the *eru* had enough wealth and prestige to have their own servants.

They stood at a crossroad. There was a red clay mound at the side of the road for those who cared to sacrifice to Esu, divinity of fate and messenger to the Creator.

"Servant of Ajayi, take my family to Ogunsanwo compound in Ogbon Oya ward," Olade's mama said tiredly. "I will leave you here."

"Where are you going, Mama?" asked Layo.

"I must go quickly to view the body of the mother of Ajayi. Then I must see that my pregnant daughter is well. After that, I will return home to begin the mask."

As she turned to go, a woman began speaking directly into her face. At first Olade's mama looked annoyed, but then her expression changed to a soft glow.

Ogunsanwo, masters of black metal,
One makes the tool that cuts the ground,
Fourmilayo, mother of Tola and Toyin,

Mother of Olade, mother of sons,
She who has grace,
Guests are ashamed to dance in her presence,
Fourmilayo, one who transforms cool mud to life.
She went to the palace; the oba received her and
turned all the less skilled away.
Fourmilayo now paints her house in many colors
  and
has a carved door on her workplace.

The praise-singer stepped back.

"No, no," said Olade's mama. "You cannot use those last words about the palace." She held cowries in her hand, but did not give them to the praise-singer. "Promise me you won't use those last words," she said.

"All right, Mother. As you wish." The woman bowed and walked away with the money.

Layo was startled. "Was it true that your work was favored at the palace? Why don't you want the words sung?"

"Yes, Layo, it is true and I am wealthy because of it. But I don't want it sung about. A woman's roles are as wife and mother. Anything beyond she mustn't brag about," Old Mama said softly. "I don't want to be accused of witchcraft."

Olade's mama stepped off to her business. The servant led them to Ogunsanwo compound. Layo was a little nervous, arriving without her grandmother.

57

The compound was very large. The outside was whitewashed. Someone had painted lines to represent a river and outlines of many water animals on the gate wall.

When they passed through the gate, Layo saw that the courtyard was paved with potsherds. The pattern, a spiral that swirled from the center to the veranda, was magnificent. Layo wondered what it represented. There were a few small bushes to mark the length of shadows and the usual goats and fowl. Many carved-and-painted posts held up the veranda roof. A shrine to a divinity held its own room. Someone was a priest or priestess here. Layo could see a second courtyard through an open doorway.

She was impressed. Her uncle, the head of this compound, must be an important man, perhaps a chief. He would greet visitors, give advice, and even hold court in his own courtyard.

The servant led them to this second smaller courtyard, which was paved with a quieter pattern—alternating rows of quartz with rows of potsherds.

There, a middle-aged man sat on a bench lined with leopard skins, his feet elevated on a footstool. He was very muscular. Layo assumed this was because her uncle's work was forging iron. His white shirt and pants and quiet expression gave him a calm, cool look. A boy sat next to him on a mat. Layo was immediately comfortable.

The servant prostrated himself, and Bisi's mama and Layo bowed deeply. "Greeting to your house, Father," said Bisi's mama.

"It will hear your greeting, Mother," the man replied.

"I am Aina, mother of Bisi, wife of Winsemi compound. We have come here with the mother of Olade to help her with her work," Bisi's mama said solemnly.

"I am Olade," the man said. "The father of Ogunkeye, husband of Ogunsanwo compound. You," he nodded to Layo, "come here." He took Layo's hand when she walked up to him. He turned her head gently, looking at her face. "Your eyes remind me of my grandmother's. Are you my sister's daughter?"

"Yes, Father," Layo said, bowing.

"This compound shall be home to you while you are here. And yours, too," he added graciously to Bisi's mama.

"Kosoko," he said to the boy. "Bring Toyin here."

The boy ran off. Layo's uncle told the servant he could go, and then asked his guests about the health of the members of their compound. He asked them if they had had a pleasant journey. He held Bisi and told him he was a handsome boy and that his papa was a great hunter.

Bisi said, "*Baba, baba.*"

Kosoko came back with a tall, slender girl who wore a clay-stained wrapper. She was smiling and her smile showed off the beauty of her face, with its wide dark eyes.

"This is my daughter, Toyin." He introduced Layo and Bisi's mama and Bisi, then said, "Show Bisi's mama the guest room and Layo, Mama's room, and help them to get acquainted."

"Yes, Papa." Toyin bowed and smiled. "This way," she said to her guests as she stepped gracefully away. She reminded Layo of Olade's mama. "You can wash after your long journey. Then we can eat some supper and go to market."

Some of the women of the compound were already cooking, and they were introduced on the way to the room. Everyone was friendly and welcoming with all the proper greetings.

"Here's your room, Mama," Toyin said in a lively voice to Bisi's mama. "If you want to leave your things, I'll show you where water is."

Bisi's mama put down her bundle in a pretty room with a green-finished floor and a colorful mat. Bisi whimpered.

"Thank you, Toyin. I'll feed the baby while you show Layo her room," she said. She sat on the mat and prepared to nurse the child.

Toyin and Layo found Olade's mama's room near the center of the compound. She was the eldest here. That she had wealth was obvious from the carved door and posts marking her room. That she had earned respect was equally obvious from

Toyin's behavior. Toyin began to speak softly when they neared the door, as if they were entering a shrine.

Layo placed her things inside the door, and Toyin bounced away.

"Let's get water and wash." She clapped her hands and stepped about in a dance.

Layo smiled at her energetic cousin. "Thank you. Then I want to see where our mama makes her terra-cottas."

Toyin smiled an even bigger smile than ever. "All right," she said enthusiastically. "You've got it, too, maybe?"

"Got what?"

"Clay in your blood."

"Clay in my blood? What does that mean?"

"You love to work clay. And you're good at it." Toyin suddenly was serious. "But all everyone wants you to do is get married and have babies, then work clay when you're old."

Layo was uncertain how to respond. She had kept her ability secret for so long. Was it safe to talk about it now?

Toyin continued, "I've got it. Clay in my blood. Some of the women don't like me, but I don't care." Toyin whispered, "They're jealous."

"Toyin!" Layo hissed. Jealousy between children and adults was taboo. One could not even speak of it. Layo was wide-eyed. "Aren't you

61

afraid someone will use witchcraft against you?"

"No, my papa has a powerful juju to protect me."

"But still, you make yourself a target."

Toyin laughed. "You sound like our mama. She says one should eat one's yam under one's hand, concealing one's wealth and ability in order to prevent envy and accusations."

"Our mama is wise," Layo said sternly.

Toyin let the subject drop.

They fetched water, and Layo and Toyin washed in a secluded spot in the compound. Then Toyin went off to care for her younger sister while her mother cooked the evening meal.

Olade's mama returned as Layo was tying on a clean wrapper. She joined the woman in the potters' area of the compound. Old Mama was selecting clay to make the mask when Layo greeted her.

"What can I do to help, Mama?"

"Bring me some of the finer potsherds, please. If you can't find any, pound up some of the coarser ones."

"Yes, Mama," she said, satisfied. This was work that she loved.

Olade's mama gathered her materials in a room and closed the door most of the way.

She had been working only a brief time when two well-dressed men arrived in the compound and asked for her. These men were very muscular and Layo wondered if they were blacksmiths, too.

She timidly went to the door of the potter's room and called to Old Mama.

Her mama came out, washed her hands, and turned to the two men who had prostrated themselves before their elder.

"Good day, Father of Obalara," Mama said.

"Greetings, Mother of Olade. We have come to ask your aid." The two men remained on the ground as they begged a favor. "As you know, we are working with the new metal, bronze. And we are attempting to make a funeral mask for the mother of Ajayi. She was a member of the *Ogboni* senate. She deserves bronze."

"Yes."

What? Layo was surprised. These men were working on the same project as her mama. Mama had competition, and she had known it, but she had given no sign when she returned to the compound. Mama didn't seem upset or worried. She remained cool. Layo was impressed.

"We would like your help," the man continued. "The head must be constructed on a clay core. You are the best. We will pay you well. Will you make this clay core for us?"

Olade's mama said, "Get up, Father of Obalara. Get up, Dada," she said to the young man with him. Dada had large natural curls in his hair. He also was handsome, Layo observed.

"You speak very kindly of my modest talents but, as you know, Father of Obalara," Olade's mama said quietly, "I too am making a funeral mask for the mother of Ajayi. I've made a commitment. That project will take all my time."

"Mother," he replied, "our bronze head is the one Ajayi compound will purchase for the funeral."

"I have seen few bronze objects and nothing this large. You propose a difficult project. You must prove yourself."

"It has been done before," he said mysteriously, "for the *oba*." He continued, "Because this is a difficult project, I want the best. I want your help."

Layo was getting angry. These men were competing with her grandmother. They wanted her help, and they had the nerve to say their mask would be better than Mama's.

Mama stayed calm. "I have faith in my medium. I will continue with my own project. Good day to you." She used that as an ending to the conversation and turned away from the men.

Layo glared at the two until the younger one glanced at her, then she bowed, as she must. He smiled at her, which just made her angrier. How dare he smile at her when she was mad at him? She glared at him again. He looked confused.

The men left and Layo looked at Mama questioningly. "They said their work will be better than yours, Mama. Doesn't that make you angry?"

"Layo, perhaps their work will be better. Bronze is quite beautiful and full of power. If they can manage the size of the piece, I've no doubt their work will be purchased over mine."

"Then why didn't you help them?"

"I would truly have liked to help them. The world is based on cooperation between men and women," she said thoughtfully. "But it is just as I've said, I have made a commitment to Ajayi compound to make a funeral mask. If I abandon my project to help with theirs and they fail . . . well, Ajayi compound would have to delay the funeral even longer, wouldn't they?

"I am wondering," she continued, "who they will get to help with their project. They need an older woman, and there aren't many of us left. . . . One last thing, Layo."

"Yes, Mama."

"You have a terrible scowl on your face. You didn't look like that when those men were here, did you? Because," she continued, "Dada is the man I want you to marry."

Chapter 7

Layo was not a happy girl. Her grandmother wanted her to marry a man she didn't like. All through the evening meal on the veranda she sat quietly. Toyin had tried to talk to her several times, but had eventually given up after receiving one too many one-word answers.

She was worried about pleasing Olade's mama and her parents. She knew her parents would be very angry if she went against her old mama's wishes.

She wasn't worried that she had ruined things with Dada. Hadn't her fortune said she would get whatever she wanted? Well, she didn't want Dada. The *babalawo* said she was supposed to do what was good for her family, not just for herself. Hadn't Dada insulted her mama? True, he hadn't spoken, but he was with the man who had said the words and he hadn't disagreed with him. That was just as bad. No, she thought defiantly, I won't do it. But how to please the adults? Somehow, she must show them what she knew: that Dada was a poor choice. She would slam the gate on him.

Her mind made up, she was able to turn her thoughts to the people around her.

"Where's Bisi's mama?" she asked, surprised when she scanned the crowd of diners and didn't see her.

Toyin looked just as surprised. "Well, she speaks."

"Oh, I'm sorry," said Layo, embarrassed when she realized she had shut out Toyin.

"Think nothing of it," said Toyin. She smiled. "I have to help clean up the place now. Then we can go sightseeing."

Layo was thrilled when she skipped with Toyin through the main gate to the road. They briefly joined a crowd watching a spectacle. Masqueraders celebrated the day of their deity with drumming and dancing.

Past that, the street was suddenly empty.

"'Most everybody's still at home," Toyin said. "Let's go see the staff of Oranmiyan."

They turned right at the crossroads. Layo marveled at the murals on one compound wall, full of painted chameleons and fish-legged men.

They soon stopped at a great cylindrical stone that was the height of at least three men. The stone was studded with iron nails.

"What's it for?" Layo asked.

"I don't know exactly. The cult of Oranmiyan is very private. The stone's been here a long time. Sometimes there are secret rituals around it with big sacrifices." Toyin shuddered, but she refused to say more.

They circled on to the palace, passing people on their way to market. Layo gasped when she saw the great gate. The wall in front of the palace was the length of many compounds and as high as a tree. She had never before seen a structure so large.

They walked and walked as they followed the wall around the palace. In places, Layo could see the crowns of big trees.

"The *oba* has his own forest inside. He can farm or go hunting there, or collect herbs for medicine," said Toyin.

"That surprises me, that a divinity would want to do those things."

"Well, the *oba* was once a human, as you know. It must be hard to leave behind the things one once did."

Layo knew that the *oba* could be either a man or a woman. He or she was chosen from a few families by the *Ogboni*. The mother of Ajayi, for whom Grandmother was making a funeral mask, had been a member of the *Ogboni*.

Layo felt touched by grandness as they left the palace walls. This palace held in it everything important to her people. She had heard that the *oba* was the ultimate judge in disputed cases. He had dozens of courtyards, many shrines full of icons, and great wealth. She imagined all the carved posts and doors, pavements, and painted walls. She also imagined the wealth of people inside. Besides the chiefs who came every day to court, there were hundreds of wives and children, the craftsmen and women, the *Ogboni* senate, the bondsmen and *eru,* and anyone who sought asylum in the *oba*'s palace. Those who were made differently, such as the lame or the blind, often lived out their lives protected there. They were created by the drunken divinity Obatala and were now sacred to him and therefore sacred to all of the people.

"It's amazing that the *oba* can keep the peace in the city. There are so many compounds," observed Layo as they headed toward the market.

"The *oba* doesn't have to deal directly with each compound," said Toyin. "The city is divided into wards. Ogunsanwo compound is in Ogbon Oya ward. Disputes between wards are resolved by ward chiefs. It's the ward chiefs who take the big problems that no one can agree upon to the *oba*."

The girls reached the evening market and tripped up and down the crowded rows of merchandise. Layo was breathless with excitement. There was mat after mat of calabash gourds and fine cloth and cheap cloth, and yams, game, vegetables, oil, chickens, salt, and pots, soap, palm wine, indigo dye, iron items, firewood, brooms, and even mats of mats for sale.

There were people packed into the space bargaining and visiting, sharing their day, children playing, and young men talking to girls of their choice. Everywhere she went, people smiled at Layo and welcomed her.

She saw the servant of the mother of Ajayi slowly walking with another man up and down the rows. Both were dressed in fine clothes and carried cutlasses. The man *was* a guard at market. That answered her question. He was *eru*. The *eru* market guards of Ife were so famous for their arrogance and power that even Layo had heard of them in far-away Abiri.

She was curious about what it was like being *eru*. To be taken from your home. But she would never ask such a question. Some people bragged about owning *eru*, but she felt that to mention a person's *eru* status would be rude and disrespectful.

She spotted Dada with a group of young men and quickly ducked behind a stall.

"What are you doing?" Toyin asked, joining her.

"See that curly-haired man over there?" she asked, pointing.

"Yes . . . that's just Dada." Toyin stepped out into the open.

"Well, I don't want him to see me."

"Why not?"

"Our mama wants me to marry him, and I don't like him."

Toyin paused. "Why not?" She sounded very puzzled. "If I weren't already betrothed . . . well, he seems quite acceptable to me."

"Well, not to me," Layo said sharply. "He insulted our mama."

"What?" Toyin hesitated only a moment, then pulled at her cousin's arm. "Come, let's go someplace quiet where we can talk."

Layo followed Toyin to a grove of trees at the edge of the market.

"It smells too bad here," said Layo. "Let's go farther away from the market."

Toyin mumbled something about country people, but she led the way past several compounds to another grove.

"Does this suit you?" Toyin asked, as she sniffed the air with great exaggeration.

Layo smiled. "It's fine." She then told Toyin about how the bronze casters had come to recruit their mama, saying that their work would be better than hers, and "Dada didn't speak out."

Toyin was properly outraged.

"What can I do? I don't want to marry Dada, but I must obey my parents."

"If we can show how bad Dada is," said Toyin, "maybe they'll change their minds. After all, he is fifteen and a man. He's old enough to speak out when he disagrees with something. By not speaking he agreed with the father of Obalara."

"Do you know anything about his compound?"

"Yes. It is in the Ita Yemoo ward on the northern edge of town. The women there make terracottas. The men are blacksmiths, but it seems that Dada has been apprenticed to the father of Obalara to work bronze."

Layo felt a pang of regret. Her mamas were trying to please her by placing her with women who worked clay. Well, it couldn't be helped. An insult was an insult. If Dada's family treated others badly, they weren't for her or her family.

"I've heard of bronze, but I've never seen it," Layo said. "What does it look like?"

"It's lighter in color than iron and it shines. I once saw it when the *Ogboni* intervened in a fight. Human blood had been shed on the earth," Toyin explained. "The *Ogboni* threw a special staff with a bronze head on the spot to mark it until the quarrel could be resolved."

Toyin switched thoughts abruptly. "Listen, Layo, I have an idea. I know a girl of the Obalufon compound, which is the compound of Obalara's father. We could go visit her."

"What? I don't want to chance getting near Dada."

"Well, how are we going to find out bad things

if we don't spy?" Toyin whispered emphatically, her excitement growing. "Maybe we could even figure out an excuse to go to the furnace outside of town."

Layo just looked at Toyin. "We could gather firewood out there for the next firing," she said thoughtfully.

"Yes!" agreed Toyin. "Ebun will take us there. She's always talking about her papa, the bronze caster. But we mustn't tell her what we're doing."

The girls were smiling as they headed back to Ogunsanwo compound. Toyin asked, "What did our mama say to the father of Obalara, anyway?"

"Oh, she was very cool. I couldn't have done it. She just said she had made a commitment. Then, when they were gone, she told me that maybe they *would* make a better mask."

"That's our mama," said Toyin. "I wish I could be as cool as she."

"Me, too," said Layo, and she meant it.

▲▲▲

Layo was alone when she woke in her old mama's room the next morning. The woman must be at work. The sun already glinted over the compound wall.

After she had washed and dressed, Layo found Toyin, who had already done her chores. The evening before, Layo had given Toyin the colorful glass beads her mother had sent. Toyin now wore them as a belt tied around her wrapper, and she was smiling. They found Toyin's mother sitting with her father in his room. The woman surprised and pleased Layo by saying her praise poem to her, then she turned to Toyin, and said,

Ogunsanwo, masters of black metal,
One makes the tool that cuts the ground,
Daughter of Olade,
One who outshines others in beauty,
Her smile lights the way before her.

Toyin's smile became even brighter.

Then Layo was struck by something, something so obvious, yet she had never thought of it before. One took the praise poem of one's father's compound. But her old mama had taken the poem of her son's compound. *Ogunsanwo* was how Olade's mama's poem started, too. Who then was Olade's mama's father?

And there was something else. She had always thought the accented tones with which Olade's mama spoke were an Ife accent, but the people here didn't speak as she did at all.

Layo suddenly had a sick feeling. She didn't want to think about this. She must shove all thoughts of it from her mind.

"Mama, may Layo and I gather firewood for

the next firing today?" Layo could see that Toyin was holding her breath.

"Yes," said her mother, her eyes sparkling. "That will give Layo a chance to see more of Ife."

The girls thanked her quickly and bowed several times on their way out.

Layo went to talk with their grandmother, who was at work on the mask.

"Mama," called Layo at the carved door of the workroom. This was the door the praise-singer sang about. Carved on it were scenes of the different stages of working clay. There were six panels, showing the digging, refining, shaping of clay, and the praising of Iya Mapo, in no particular order, as well as the finished products of jars, jugs, and terra-cottas.

"Yes, Layo," answered Old Mama from within.

"The mother of Toyin has said we may gather firewood today, for the next firing. May I do that?"

"Yes," said her mama, with a sigh.

"Thank you, Mama." Layo felt bad. Going off with Toyin was was not helping in the way she said she would. She wanted to stay and help Olade's mama with the clay and Bisi's mama with Bisi. But if she didn't do something, she might have to spend her whole life with Dada. She must go.

"Layo," Olade's mama said as she came out of the room.

"Yes, Mama?"

"Have you seen my wooden cutter? I can't seem to find it."

"No, Mama," Layo said, surprised. "I'll help you look for it."

"I have looked everywhere already. I shall have to make another. My work will be delayed until this afternoon."

"Oh, I'm sorry, Mama. Should I stay and help?"

"No, there is nothing you can do. Go and gather your firewood."

Layo bowed and backed away. This was troubling. Her grandmother's tools had been disturbed once before. Was someone using witchcraft against Olade's mama? Perhaps the tools were cursed.

On the way out the gate they met Bisi's mama.

"Good morning, girls," she said, in a dignified way that Layo had never heard from her before. "Try the beancakes from the vendor down the road," she said, as she showed them the food wrapped in a leaf. "They are delicious."

Bisi had a beancake in one hand and was cheerfully smearing it on his face and his mother's back as he fed himself.

"I will, thank you," Layo said. "We are gathering firewood today. Will you be able to help Mama and take care of Bisi?"

"Yes," Bisi's mama said generously. "Go, and make sure you see the city along the way."

"Thank you, Mama." Layo bowed again and turned away. She wasn't sure she liked people thinking she was sightseeing instead of working. She wasn't sightseeing, but she couldn't tell them she was *spying*. That was even worse!

Chapter 8

THEY PAID A FEW COWRIES for some of the fried beancakes that Bisi's mama had recommended. They munched their breakfast as they walked.

The two girls, dressed in faded blue work wrappers, arrived at Obalufon compound, which was at the edge of the city. They entered the compound gates and asked for Ebun.

They found Ebun helping her mother prepare her loom. Women's cloth was wider and shorter than men's, so it was possible to set up the loom on the veranda.

Toyin and Layo bowed, and Toyin said to Ebun's mama, "We've come to do you a favor." Layo was surprised. She wondered what favor she would be performing.

"Oh?" asked Ebun's mama.

"Yes. Layo, who is my cousin from Abiri," Toyin said, gesturing toward Layo, "and I are gathering firewood today for the next firing of pots. Ebun can earn money if she comes with us and gathers firewood. My mama will pay the market rate."

"My, that is generous. Ebun, do you want to do this?"

"Yes, Mama." The small girl nodded. Ebun was ten.

"Toyin, you are responsible for Ebun then," the woman reminded her.

"Yes, Mama."

Layo spotted Dada as she turned to go. He and the father of Obalara were at work carving what looked like beeswax. Dada looked away when she saw him. At least he is not rude enough to stare, she thought. He turned his attention to the work of the father of Obalara. The object was the size and shape of a head. So, they made not just a mask but a full head. And who had made the clay core? Layo wondered.

"Thank you, Elder, for thinking of me for this work," Ebun said, with a little bow to Toyin as they headed toward the gate.

"Well, you are welcome, Ebun, but first, I am thirsty. Do you think we could sit and have some water before we begin?"

"Of course."

Ebun got three small gourds, and the girls sat in the shade of the veranda near Ebun's mama. Toyin slyly nudged Layo and nodded toward Dada. Layo gave an answering nod. Yes, she knew this was just a way to watch Dada.

They sat as long as they could, but the time was not very fruitful. Dada mostly watched the father of Obalara, and sometimes he fetched tools. He was very attentive, which obviously was what was expected of him. Certainly nothing they observed showed that Dada was a bad choice for marriage.

Once in a while, Dada glanced their way. Layo made a point of sipping water then. Dada was very handsome. He was a hard worker. And there were potters in his compound. Layo began to regret her decision. "We had better go," she said, then whispered, "I think we are starting to look suspicious."

Toyin nodded and got up.

"Ebun, the work your papa's doing looks interesting," said Toyin, as they left the compound.

"Yes, he is going to cast a bronze head," she said proudly.

"Oh really," said Layo. "I don't know anything about that. Just how is that done?"

Ebun said eagerly, "Papa will carve and carve wax until it looks like the mother of Ajayi. Then he'll pour in the hot bronze. Lots of steam and hot wax squirts out."

"I don't understand, Ebun," said Layo. "How does the metal keep its shape?"

"Oh, the wax was molded onto a clay core that someone made for Papa. When he finishes carving," Ebun said importantly, "the wax will be very thin, like a piece of heavy cloth. When that's done, more clay will be molded on top of the wax. The clay makes a container that keeps the shape of the carved wax. After the pouring, the clay mold will be broken away."

"Thank you, Ebun," said Layo. "Now I understand. Who, I wonder, made the clay core?"

"Elder, I don't know. That task was completed this morning before I arose."

They collected many loads of firewood and delivered them home. Though she knew Dada was at Obalufon compound, Layo looked around for him each time they arrived back in the city with their bundles perched on their heads. She was eager to find fault with him, but there were no more glimpses of Dada.

By evening, Toyin made sure a weary Ebun arrived safely home at Obalufon's compound. When Layo and Toyin returned to their compound, they saw that Mama had finished molding the mask and had set it out to dry.

Of course Layo and Toyin didn't touch it. They just sat awhile and looked at it. Layo imagined the reddish mask with painted features.

The mask revealed the face of a serene, strong woman, one who embodied calmness. The figure was of a person in her middle years.

"I didn't know she was so young," Layo said to Olade's mama, who rested on the mat next to them.

"She wasn't. I represented her at the height of her life."

"Oh. Mama, how could you work so quickly? Your cutter was missing only this morning."

"Well, in addition to that, I was a little distracted. Soon my daughter will give birth, and I will go to her compound to take care of her. Once I was able to put that out of my mind, I devised a replacement cutter. The work did go quickly then.

"Gathering materials always takes the most time for these projects," continued Mama. "Getting the tools together, getting just the right clay, then mixing it to the right consistency. While I'm preparing those things, I try to envision the finished work. That seems to be my special ability. To know what the object will look like before I even begin, and to envision each step of the work, as well. I rarely have to try again and again," she said thoughtfully. "I have always been like that. I am very fortunate."

Layo thought back to the pot she had made in Abiri. She had seen what it would look like before she had even begun. And she had wondered where the ability to do that had come from.

The girl put her arms around her old mama to share the joy she felt. Her spirits soared in the returned hug.

Toyin smiled at them, knowingly.

▲▲▲

The next day Layo, Toyin, and Ebun went again to spy on Dada, though Ebun didn't know she was spying. She just went along with whatever her elders did.

Along the edges of the forest, they gathered pieces of wood and bundled them with twine to carry on their heads into the city.

"Let's show Layo the furnace," Toyin said to Ebun, once on their way back to Ogunsanwo compound. Ebun, who as youngest led the way, nodded and took a different fork in the path. They walked single file through the woods, bearing their loads of firewood. When Ebun spotted a big dome through the trees, she put down her load.

"See," she said to Layo, pointing at the dome.

Of course Layo had seen a furnace before, but she pretended to be very interested. Layo and Toyin dropped their firewood, too. The three girls approached the dome, which was formed from mud that had dried and hardened in the hot sun.

Dada was there with some other men his age. They were digging ashes from the furnace from a previous firing. Dada looked their way, and Layo and the girls bowed. Layo was grim-faced. Dada acknowledged their presence with a nod and returned to work.

"There's an underground tunnel from the dome that is the length of several men," explained Ebun. "It helps create a draft to make a really hot fire. It's around here somewhere, so be careful you don't fall into it."

"Thank you. Here it is," said Layo, as she carefully walked around a hole in the ground. She regretted that Dada was working hard. She had hoped that she would find him sitting and talking to his friends, or even better, playing in the forest.

They picked up their loads of firewood and headed for Ogunsanwo compound. The wall around the city had not yet extended here, so they did not have to search for the gate.

They heard thunder and looked around for shelter.

"There's a farm hut," said Ebun. Big drops of rain began to pelt them, and they ran to the house. They bent over to enter the low door and dragged their firewood in after them to keep it dry, too. Toyin pulled the woven, wood door shut after them.

The rain came down in a torrent, as it always did, while lightning flashed above. They sat snug and dry in the small dark shelter.

"I wish Dada would pay attention to me," said Ebun.

"Why?" asked Layo, startled.

Ebun was equally startled that Layo would have to ask. "Elder, he is the oldest son in his compound. If I were his wife," said Ebun dreamily, "I would be boss of all his future wives and all the wives of his younger brothers."

Toyin and Layo looked at each other.

Ebun continued, "My mama says they have many people in a wide circle of friendships, as well as money."

"But the women there are potters. Don't you want to weave like your own mama?" Layo asked.

"Oh, that's not important, is it? I could learn to work clay or anything." She smiled brightly.

Layo rested her chin in her hands. The other girls talked, but she did not listen.

Layo felt confused. Dada looked more attractive all the time. She sighed. She still wanted to find a flaw to avenge the insult against her mama. There was the problem. There weren't any flaws that she could see. He worked hard. He had good health. He obeyed his elders. And he had that finely formed body and those wonderful large curls in his hair.

"I don't know. She does this sometimes," Layo heard Toyin say.

"Who does what?" Layo asked.

"You. Your eyes glaze over and you don't hear what anyone says," Toyin informed her.

"Oh." Layo smiled a crooked little smile. "I guess I do do that. The rain has stopped," she said, listening. "Let's go."

They dragged their bundles of firewood out of the hut, helped Ebun to lift hers, and were on their way again on the path through the forest. The air smelled fresh and earthy from the rain.

Layo took deep breaths, and felt a little homesick. The forest reminded her of home. Wherever one stood in the village of Abiri, the woods were within a few steps. She liked the excitement of the city but, she decided, she liked a village better. Her pleasure in living in Abiri lay beyond the fact that it was familiar. The surrounding forest was like a magic cloth. It protected her like a juju. *It* was her home.

The path was muddy from the heavy rain. Layo could feel the cool mud ooze up between her toes. She liked the squishy feel of it. She began to slap her feet down to hear the *plash!* they made.

"Layo, you're getting your legs and wrapper all muddy," Toyin said.

"I am sacrificing to Iya Mapo," Layo answered and continued.

Suddenly, *pit, splat* could be heard coming from Ebun's feet.

"Oh, well," said Toyin, as she joined in the sacrificial act, all the way home.

They left their wood in the potter's area. Layo glanced into the workroom. Old Mama had fired the funeral mask and had left it sitting in her workroom.

Toyin got some cowries and paid Ebun for her bundle, just as she had promised the girl's mother. Ebun went to talk to some girls of her own age in the compound.

"This is getting expensive," complained Toyin. "I'm running out of cowries. I already broke open my bank. Do you have any money?"

It had been a lie that Toyin's mama would pay. The two girls had to come up with the money themselves.

"I have a few cowries," Layo answered softly,

"from the sale of the pots my mama sent with me. They won't last long, but I'll get them."

Before she could do so, though, Toyin's mama called to them. When they entered her room, she took one look and said, "Oh, just look at you. Go wash. Then, for the rest of the afternoon, I want you to stay here to work."

"Yes, Mama," said Toyin, as she bowed.

"Mama," Layo asked, "where is my mama?"

"Her daughter has given birth, and Mama is caring for her."

Layo helped the women make pottery, but she was disappointed she couldn't go out again to spy.

"Toyin, I'm worried," Layo said as they fetched water to work the clay. "We won't be allowed to leave much more to gather firewood."

"Well, Mama didn't say we couldn't gather any more firewood. She just said to stay here today."

"That's true, but we'll soon have to stay here to work with our mothers. Tomorrow, we must find out something."

Chapter 9

"TODAY I FEEL like the trickster tortoise," Toyin said. "We will be sly and spy on Dada and get our way."

"Sometimes the tortoise is caught and punished for his wily ways," said Layo as they traveled to get Ebun. Spying was still in the day's plan.

"You worry too much. What could happen?" asked Toyin.

Layo shrugged as they entered the gate of Obalufon compound. They found Ebun and told her they wanted to see bronze casting.

The three girls found Dada at the furnace outside of town. Several men, including Dada, loaded wood and the crucible with metal in it into the furnace.

Ebun said the metal wouldn't be ready to pour until the shadows were long in the afternoon, so the girls gathered firewood all day, but did not take it home. Ebun understood that they might not be able to return to the furnace if they did. She wanted to see the pouring, too. They returned in time to see the men open the smoking furnace.

"Ebun, girls, stand back," said her papa, the father of Obalara. They all moved away.

He took the crucible out with iron tongs. The mold of the head of the mother of Ajayi sat braced in the dirt close by. The man carefully poured the hot metal. Suddenly, with a loud pop, hot metal erupted and sprayed. The men leaped back and dove to the ground as the mold exploded.

"Ogun, bless us," said the father of Obalara. "Is anyone burned?"

Calls of *no* came from all around as the would-be bronze casters picked themselves up off the ground.

"Some of the casting sprues must have failed," muttered the father of Obalara. "We must begin again."

"What's a casting sprue?" Layo asked Ebun.

"It's a tunnel of wax. When you pour the hot metal in, it's supposed to melt, to let the hot gases escape."

"You know so much, Ebun. Why don't you become a bronze caster?" Layo teased.

Ebun stared at her. "I could become a bronze caster if I wanted to."

"Yes, but then," Layo said quietly, "people would whisper that you are a witch."

Ebun nodded solemnly in agreement.

"Someone did a pretty careless job on that mold. I never have that kind of problem when my work's fired," Toyin said, matter-of-factly. "Some women's pots crack or even explode because they don't dry them enough before firing. Mine never break, because I'm so skillful."

Both girls stared at Toyin in surprise. They had never before heard a female go on so about her ability.

Then Layo said, "Yes, and you are so humble."

"I told you I don't worry. I have a juju my papa gave me."

"It's a good thing, too," Layo said.

▲▲▲

That evening at market—Toyin had been sent by her mama to bargain for soap—the girls spotted Dada with a group of young men his age. They were all washed and dressed in fine clothes, ready to court their betrothed at market.

"Let's go around here and listen from behind that stall," said Toyin.

Layo agreed, but stopped to look at goods along the way. The stall was full of calabashes that were carved with marvelous figures and shapes.

As she followed one carved spiral with her finger, she heard one of the young men say, "You are very popular, Dada. The girls don't wait for you to approach them at market; they come to watch you even at work."

"Yes, Dada, it looks as though you could have yourself an aggressive woman."

They all laughed, except Dada.

"Toyin is betrothed," said another, "but that Layo, that dark, pretty little village girl—she could be yours. I've no doubt that she'll soon ask you."

The men roared with laughter, even Dada.

Layo felt her face burning with rage or shame, she didn't know which. She found herself running alone through the market. She dodged people and mats and stalls. She ran down an aisle between mats of cloth. She tripped over a pile. She caught herself. She ran on.

A hand clamped onto her shoulder. Her body jerked sharply as her feet kept trying to run.

"Stop, I command you, in the name of the *oba*."

Layo twisted around and saw a market guard. His huge hand was on her shoulder. He was the same man she had seen walking with the servant of the mother of Ajayi.

"Yes, yes. I stop," she said as she tried to wriggle out from his grip.

"You have to hold still before I'll let go," he said, calmly. "And don't run off again."

Layo, her blood racing, forced herself to be still.

The guard loosened his grip slowly, as if ready to clamp his hand back on her again if she made any sudden moves.

"Now walk. Don't run about like a little child."

She swallowed this insult because she *had* been running about like a little child.

"Father, where is the servant of the house of the mother of Ajayi?" she asked, looking around.

"He is ill. He has *iba*."

"Oh." Almost everybody got *iba* at one time or another, and sometimes people died from it. "I hope that he gets well," Layo said. "I will walk now." She bowed and the guard walked away.

"There you are," said Toyin, striding up. "Weren't they awful? Well, the trick's on them. They think you're interested in Dada. If they only knew that we were really trying to get you out of marrying him. Ha!"

"I think we've probably succeeded," said Layo. It had been what she'd wanted. Why did she feel so bad now? Layo felt suddenly tired. She hung her head as she walked home.

There was a commotion when they entered through the compound gate. There was their grandmother, standing in the middle of the main courtyard, yelling. The old woman made gestures to the air, since there didn't seem to be any particular person around to yell at.

"I will discover the criminal. And when I do you will not get away with it. You will be beaten!" and so on and over again ranted the woman.

"What has happened?" Layo asked Kosoko,

who was standing wide-eyed on the veranda next to her.

"The mask our mama made was smashed, and her tools are gone *again*."

"Oh! Witchcraft?" she said softly to Toyin.

"No!" Olade's mama yelled at her. The startled Layo flinched. "Witchcraft causes illness and death. Witches just think bad things, and they happen, with the aid of certain objects," Olade's mama said more calmly. "This was a criminal!" she said, her voice rising sharply. "Someone destroyed my work and took my things. Someone has wanted to stop my work."

"Mother," called Ogunkeye's papa as he entered the compound. "I have heard. I will begin an investigation immediately. Come to my courtyard. I will question everyone. We will find an answer."

Mama led the way to his courtyard. The head of the compound took his seat on the leopard skins, seating his mother on the bench beside him.

All the residents of the compound had left their work and gathered round out of interest. Ogunkeye's papa spoke to them.

"We shall begin an investigation of the disappearance of our mother's tools and the destruction of her work. Please, Mama, first describe these tools."

"There are two items missing: a wooden knife, consecrated—I called a spirit to it; and a simple bark scraper, like any a woman making pots would use.

"The trouble began with the tools being tossed about in Abiri. I recovered them then and thought the goats had done it."

"Perhaps they did," said Ogunkeye's papa.

"Yes, perhaps. But I have lost two of each from the workroom since returning to Ife."

Ogunkeye's papa asked, "Has any little child found these things as playthings?" He said gently to the children gathered in front of him on the ground, "If one of you has these things, return them now. Don't be afraid. You won't be punished," he promised. He looked around, resting his gaze on the more ornery ones. No one volunteered.

"Mama," continued Ogunkeye's papa, "what did you use these tools for?"

"I made a funeral mask for the mother of Ajayi. I found the mask in pieces when I went to deliver it."

"Is it possible? Who did not want you to make the mask?"

"I do not know," said Mama.

"Please, Mama." Layo found it was her own voice saying that. "May I speak?"

"Yes, of course, Layo."

Layo was certain she knew who the criminals were. She bowed low before speaking. "Two weeks ago, on the day we arrived here in Ife, the bronze casters came to speak to you."

"How do you know?" asked Ogunkeye's papa. "Were you there?"

"Yes, Father. I know this to be true because I witnessed it." She continued, "The bronze casters wanted you to set aside your work and help them. You refused to help them, and the father of Obalara said their funeral mask would be better than yours. His apprentice did not disagree with him," she added.

"Well," said Ogunkeye's papa, "that is very interesting. They wanted my mother's help, but didn't get it. Has anyone here seen either of these men return to the compound?"

Layo and Toyin looked at each other, perhaps sharing the same thought. He had not even mentioned the insult. Had it not been as bad as they had thought?

Silence answered Ogunkeye's papa's question.

"We have no evidence there, then. We will continue with other questions. We must consider. Perhaps the missing tools and destroyed mask are separate crimes."

Mama was shaking, Layo noticed. That was peculiar. She hadn't seemed angry anymore.

"Mama, are you ill?" said Ogunkeye's papa, when he saw his mother's violent shivering. He touched her face.

"You have a fever." He said to Kosoko, "Hurry! Run and get the *babalawo*."

He carried his mama to her room, as Layo and Toyin followed. He said, "I promise you, Mama, I will continue this investigation until we have found and punished the culprit."

Chapter 10

THEY SPOKE LITTLE and only for necessary things.

Mama had *iba*. The *babalawo* said she must have stood out in the sun too long. That must be true. Her fever was rising and rising.

Layo stayed by Old Mama's side. The *babalawo* had gone for medicine, but he couldn't give it to Mama until this bout was over. She would just vomit it.

Mama lay naked on her mat. She moaned from the pain of the fever and headache. Along with others, Layo wrung out clean cloths in cool spring water and placed them on Mama's hot, dry body. They must keep the fever from rising too high. Fever could kill.

Layo stayed throughout the evening. A steady stream of people came to help. Toyin joined her for hours at a time. Someone kept the jar of cool water fresh.

Then Mama began to sweat, and the people began to talk. Her sweat soaked the mat. Someone brought another fresh, dry cloth.

"Oh, I am feeling better," said Olade's mama. "My head felt as if it were going to explode. Water, please."

They gave her water. She soaked everything again with her sweat, and they brought more fresh cloth.

Near morning, Mama slept. Layo lay down on a mat beside her and slept, too.

"Layo, wake up," a voice whispered.

"Go away," Layo mumbled into the thick air.

"Layo, wake up," the voice insisted. A hand shook her.

"Huh?" Layo opened her eyes. Bisi's mama knelt next to her.

"Poor child," she said softly. "I'm sorry, but you must wake up and come with me."

Layo sat up. One of the women of the compound sat next to Olade's mama. She nodded to Layo and gestured to her to be silent.

Layo followed Bisi's mama outside. The sky was lightening over the courtyard, but the sun had not yet risen.

Layo's body ached for sleep. Her head pounded and her mouth was dry. She stumbled on the veranda and leaned against the post.

"What's going on?" she asked, trying to make her tongue work.

"The father of this compound makes good on his promise to pursue the matter of the missing tools. We must go to the compound of the ward chief and be prepared to answer her questions."

"Oh," Layo cried. "I am so tired." She was nearly in tears.

"I will help you," said her mother's co-wife. "I will fetch you water to drink and to wash in. That will make you feel a little better."

Bisi's mama retrieved Bisi from a little girl who was entertaining him and set off for water. Layo made a trip to a strip of woods, every step reminding her of her exhaustion.

After she had washed and drunk and feasted on the roasted yam that Bisi's mama brought her, Layo did feel a little better. A bleary-eyed Toyin joined them and they followed Toyin to the ward chief's compound.

The ward chief, an old woman wearing blue glass beads, was waiting in her courtyard, sitting enthroned on a stone stool. Layo felt confident that this woman would find the culprit. Only fair and thoughtful people who knew how to deal with others were chosen as chiefs.

Ogunkeye's papa sat on a long bench with other chiefs, all of them dressed in white.

Everyone else sat on mats on the paved courtyard.

"This court will begin," the ward chief said.

Ogunkeye's papa rose and explained the problem of the smashed mask and the missing tools. He talked about how the problem began in Abiri and continued in Ife. He explained how his mother was ill right now, and that he would speak for her.

"If this problem began in Abiri," said one of the chiefs next to Ogunkeye's papa, "and continued here, then we must consider the people who have traveled here with the mother of Olade."

Layo was shocked. This idea woke her up.

"Who traveled here from Abiri?" asked the chief.

Ogunkeye's papa answered, "Five people traveled the path from Abiri." He named them, including Bisi.

"Send for the servant, so that we may question him," the ward chief commanded.

"He has died," Ogunkeye's papa said, "of *iba*."

Layo felt sad for him, and afraid, too. She was afraid for her old mama. She wasn't well yet. The fever could come again and again.

"Mother of Bisi, did you witness the activities of the servant of the mother of Ajayi while in Abiri?"

"No, I was preparing for the journey."

"He couldn't have done anything, Mama," Layo blurted out. "He was talking to the girls of the village while I fetched water for him to wash in. He was telling everyone that he was a market guard."

"Who are you?" asked the chief.

The girl gazed at the ground. "I am Layo. I was there, too."

"Continue, then."

"Later, though," said Bisi's mama thoughtfully, "when we were getting our things together, he might have had the chance."

"Yes. That's true," agreed Layo. "The girls went to work and he was on his own. But why would he do such a thing?"

"Why indeed?" asked the ward chief. "I believe when we discover why this thing was done, we will find out who did it."

"Yes, I agree," said Ogunkeye's papa. "So why was this done? Why destroy my mother's work?"

"Who would want to destroy her work?" asked another.

"Layo, tell us what you witnessed," said Ogunkeye's papa.

Layo got up and bowed to her elders. "The father of Obalara and his apprentice came to our compound and asked for Mama's help. She refused. They said their mask would be chosen instead of hers anyway."

There was a little stir when Layo mentioned his apprentice.

One of the chief's said, "Layo, how have you been spending your time in the city?"

"I have been gathering firewood for the firing of pottery."

"Is that what your elders asked you to do?" the chief asked.

"They didn't object, Father."

"Your mama didn't chide you for running all over the city?"

"No, Father."

"Not the least little comment? Something that might have made you angry with her?"

"No, Father." What did this mean, wondered Layo. Did the ward chief think that she had destroyed her own mama's work? She wanted to shout, *Never would I do such a thing!*

Ogunkeye's papa interrupted, saying seriously, "I have heard of no arguments between either Layo or Bisi's mama and my mother."

The ward chief sighed. "Let us then turn our attention to the father of Obalara."

"I asked him to be here," said Ogunkeye's papa. "You see the result." He swept his hand around to emphasize the absence of the father of Obalara.

"He lives in another ward. I must meet with his ward chief to discuss this matter. We will meet again." The ward chief thus abruptly ended the session.

Layo and the others returned to their compound to find Mama sitting on the veranda. She was not her usual energetic self. She struggled to drink the medicine the *babalawo* had given her.

"Ah, Layo," the old woman said. "You stayed by my side. And you, Toyin, I remember you were there, too. This medicine is so bitter. It's hard to

102

get it down." She then pinched her nose shut, tilted her head back, and gulped all the liquid from the gourd at once. Mama gagged when she was done.

"I do hope that will keep me from another bout," she said weakly.

Toyin and Bisi's mama left, saying they needed to get to work.

It hurt Layo to see her mama like this. And it made her think. She stayed to talk.

"Mama, I have some questions. Do you have the energy to talk? Should I wait until the evening?"

"No, questions can't wait," Mama said. She couldn't say, "I may die." Words held the power to make things come true. But they both knew.

The old woman put out her arms and Layo slipped into her embrace. Mama stroked her hair, and Layo cried a little. After a while, when Layo was quiet, Mama asked, "Now, what are your questions?"

Mama still held her, and Layo didn't look at her. She chose her words carefully. They were difficult to say. "I have been wondering. I never thought about it before I got here. You use the praise poem of your son's compound." She took a deep breath and said, "What is the poem of your father's compound?"

Without hesitation, Olade's mama answered with strange words, words Layo didn't understand.

Layo looked up at her grandmother. "You were *eru*?"

"I will not treat you as if you were a stranger. I will tell you. Our family has heard it and keeps it secret. I was *eru*."

Layo sighed. Though she felt again how tired she was, it was good to hear this secret. It made her feel very close to Mama, that she was willing to tell her something so personal.

"Most of the people who witnessed that are dead. Soon, no one will know for certain that it is true." Mama's voice grew stronger. "At first I was terrified and I missed my mother so much. But, as you can imagine, it is easier for a woman to be *eru*. She enters the compound and immediately becomes like any other wife. Her children become part of the family. She is no longer *eru*. For me, in certain ways, I had advantages I wouldn't have had among my own people. I do not believe I would have developed my skills in terra-cotta back in my little village. And I wouldn't give up my family here now." She stroked Layo's cheek.

"For a man who is *eru*, life is different, more difficult," she continued. "If he works very hard and saves cowries, he can purchase his freedom. If not, or if misfortune befalls him, he remains *eru*, and his children are *eru*. Those children can purchase themselves or become part of our people by being especially loved, but it can take generations."

Mama said angrily, "We who have been *eru* keep it secret. People will use it against you, Layo, not because we are inferior, but because we are strangers. We are different, having grown up with a different way of life."

For a moment, Mama was strong again. "People take difference and make it bad. They do it because they are looking for any advantage. They put others down to keep themselves ahead. People want to keep us strangers as an advantage for themselves—so, though we are now free people, they whisper about us behind our backs."

Layo thought of Kemi back in Abiri, laughing at her and her mama. "Yes, I understand," she said.

"But Mama," she asked, her curiosity rising. "How did you become *eru*?"

"My village was conquered by Yoruba chiefs looking for new followers in the forest."

Layo was shocked. Her people were always so kind.

"The Yoruba needed goods and money to build this great city of Ife. Several chiefs led a battle against my village to obtain tribute. We were defeated, and the men captured in battle became *eru*. Rather than flee the village, abandoning it forever, my people agreed to pay the tribute demanded. Two young girls were also given in tribute. I was one of those girls.

"I have come to believe that that was part of my fate. It is so strange. I sacrificed, and a bad thing turned out well. I am eager to see what the rest of my life will bring."

Chapter 11

MAMA WAS EXHAUSTED and went to sleep on her mat. Layo joined her to keep watch, but was soon asleep herself.

When Layo woke, Olade's mama was gone. She jumped up to look for her and found her in her workroom, singing as she formed the clay on a wooden board on her lap.

"Mama, should I go?" Layo asked, feeling she had interrupted a sacred act.

"No, child. Stay, I have a question for *you.*"

Layo's stomach jumped. She stood uneasily. Did Olade's mama also think she had smashed the mask?

"I have recently observed that Bisi's mama could not form a decent pot if the *oba* himself demanded it." Her smile played gently with the lines of her face. "Yet in Abiri she had in her possession a pot finely formed, strong, even, and lightweight, with a beauty to match any I have ever seen." Her face turned solemn. "Do you know anything about that pot?"

Layo was proud to hear her mama talk about her pot in this way. But what did Mama want her to say? Oh—that was easy.

"No, Mama."

"That makes me happy." Mama paused. It seemed as if she was looking at thoughts deep within. "There is in my family," she continued, "an ability to form clay. My own mother had it, as I seem to, and Toyin has it.

"Toyin. That one will run into trouble," Mama said. "She seeks trouble as though it is a mark of honor. Silly child. If one constantly challenges the power of others, as she does when she flaunts her ability, one day one will meet someone with greater power. The consequences can be illness or death for oneself or one's family through witch-craft.

"With Toyin's challenging," Mama continued, "she sets herself apart. There are many other young girls with ability. They just realize that their abiltiy is not diminished by being modestly con-cealed.

"Toyin should accept that and set her ability aside for a while. She needs to get married and have children, for people are our wealth—not things or money. Childbearing is a woman's power and brings us honor."

Mama's words went through and through Layo's mind. *There are many others.* Layo pic-tured all the other girls sneaking off into the woods to build pots or weave cloth. She smiled, not because it had been a silly thing to do, but because she now knew she was not alone.

"Mama?"

"Yes, child."

"May I watch you work?"

"Yes, for a while. Fetch some more water for me. The clay is drying."

▲▲▲

While they worked together, forces outside of them gathered. The ward chiefs had met. They argued.

"You want me to interrupt the great work of the father of Obalara on the word of a child?" said one.

"Yes. She has the backing of Olade, the father of Ogunkeye," said the other.

"No, I will not," the first replied.

"There is only one way to resolve this. We shall ask the *oba* to decide."

▲▲▲

Layo's heart began to pound when she opened the door to the man who was loudly rapping there. Half of his head was shaven from front to back. He wore a cutlass at his waist. This was a messenger from the *oba*. He prostrated himself before Mama.

"The *oba* greets you and demands that you

attend his court today." And he said, "Bring the girl Layo."

"I return his greeting, and I obey." Olade's mama bowed to the messenger as if he himself were the *oba*.

"Layo, I have been sleeping," Mama said quickly. "What did you tell the ward chief?"

"I told her about the bronze casters and their challenge to you."

"Oh, Layo. I hope you have not ruined your chances with Dada. I have cultivated a friendship with his family for years for your sake."

"But Mama, if they have ruined your work, would you, should you be silent about that?"

"No, of course not. But that's just it. I'm not so certain they have. Oh, I do wish Olade had not pursued this outside the family," she said mysteriously. "But I was too ill to tell him to stop."

"Well, there's nothing to do about it now. Let's hurry and wash and dress. One can't be late for the *oba*'s court."

▲▲▲

They entered the palace wearing their finest clothes. Olade's mama wore her wrapper with swirling patterns and a matching cloth wrapped around her head. And there was a surprise for Layo. Olade's mama had taken from a wooden box more of the same cloth for a wrapper and headcloth for Layo. She wore them with delight.

110

A guard led the way through a maze of various courts. Layo passed a group of blind people who pounded yams using big mortars and pestles. They sang to make the work go easier.

Several men sat on the veranda carving a new wood door. Layo could see lively shapes emerging from the wood. She felt the carvers drew on the power of the spiritual world very well. "Mama," she asked, "did you come here to make terra-cottas?"

"Yes. Now forget about that. We have arrived."

They had reached a large court lined with people. Along one side were chiefs in white, sitting on a long bench. Ogunkeye's papa and the ward chief were there. So was the father of Obalara, also a chief. Two men with drums stood to the side of the veranda. Olade's mama and Layo sat on a mat on the pavement. Dada, Bisi's mama, and Toyin and many others she recognized were there as well.

Layo had never seen such a lovely sight as all the people in their finest clothes of blue or white, set against the terra-cotta color of the pavement and the whitewashed walls, with the brilliant blue sky over all.

As she admired the scene, she noticed a screen on the veranda. Light shone through the screen, silhouetting a figure. Layo stiffened when she realized that a man was sitting there, a man wearing a crown.

"Mama, is that the *oba*?" she whispered.

"Yes," Olade's mama answered quietly.

Layo could see that the crown concealed the king's face. Strings of beads hung down and acted as a mask.

"Does the crown protect us from the *oba*'s power?"

"Yes. That, but it also reminds us all that power lies in the crown and in the people, not just in the person who wears it."

"Ooh."

The two drummers played a short rhythm.

A strange voice said from behind the screen, "Let us begin."

All were silent. Then the ward chief stood up and greeted the *oba* and the people in the crowd. She explained the reason for being here, the crime of the destruction of the mask and the theft of the tools.

Someone tapped Layo on the shoulder. She jumped a little and jerked around to see who it was. Ebun crouched next to her.

"Sit down and listen, Ebun," Layo whispered sternly.

"Elder, you asked me a question before. I have the answer," Ebun announced proudly.

"Quiet, Ebun, your elders are speaking," ordered Layo as she gestured to the chiefs before her.

Ebun sat on the mat and sulked.

The ward chief was going on about the importance of their great city and the steps necessary to keep it great.

"All right, Ebun," Layo said softly, "what question did I ask you before?"

Ebun turned eagerly. "You asked me who made the clay core for the mold of the head of the mother of Ajayi."

Olade's mama shushed both girls now.

Layo was stricken at not being able to know the answer, and Ebun was quietly pleased with herself for getting Layo's interest.

When Ebun looked at her Layo mouthed the word, *who?*

Olade's mama swatted Layo. She felt the eyes of everyone around her were upon her. That was the end of that.

Olade's mama was speaking now, telling her story simply and quickly. She mentioned nothing about the bronze casters.

Next, Layo was called. She felt so uncertain now. What should she say?

She told them about the bronze casters that day that now seemed so long ago.

The chief of the father of Obalara's ward took up the questioning. "So, child, how did it make you feel when they said they could make a better mask?"

Layo's heart thumped. Was everything to come out?

"I was angry. I felt my mama had been insulted," Layo said firmly, looking around at the crowd.

"You were angry," he repeated. "Well, an insult to one's mother is serious. What did you do?"

"I followed them. I watched the bronze casters work, looking for a flaw."

Layo heard her mama gasp.

"A flaw? Something to use against them, I suppose. Did you find anything?"

"No," she said in a very little voice.

"So," he said, suddenly very loudly, "being angry and wanting revenge against the bronze casters, you smashed your own mama's work and stole her tools, then started an outcry against the father of Obalara."

"No!" cried a voice from the crowd. Layo turned to see who was speaking. "I can't allow you to persecute this child," said Bisi's mama, standing up awkwardly with Bisi. "She did not do those things."

"How do you know this?" asked the muffled voice from behind the screen.

"Because," Bisi's mama began to weep, "it was I. I stole the tools and smashed the mask."

How could she? thought Layo, her anger rising. The *oba* then asked the question Layo wanted answered.

"Why?"

114

"Why?" Bisi's mama said sharply, getting control of her tears. "I was angry. It was assumed that when the great mother of Olade wanted me to come here," she said contemptuously, "I wanted to come. No one ever asked. They just assumed I was coming. I did not want to come. I am not good at working clay. But I came, hoping to improve my work."

She continued solemnly, "My work did not improve. So when the father of Obalara asked me, the apprentice of the mother of Olade, to make the clay core, I saw my chance to be a part of something great. It was a simple task that even I could perform. I made the clay core."

Ebun tapped Layo's leg and nodded.

Sounds of amazement went around the crowd. The power in such a thing could kill a young woman.

"All went well until the casting process failed," Bisi's mama went on. "We needed time to make another, and the mother of Olade was completing her work rapidly. At first, in Abiri, I scattered the tools because I was angry. Then I stole the tools here in Ife for the same reason. Finally, I smashed the mask and stole the tools to gain time. The father of Obalara did not know," she cried. "I wanted my work to succeed for a change."

Bisi's mama had begun to shake. "But I could not allow you to punish Layo. That is going too far. She is a child and I must protect her." The woman shivered violently now. "Besides, she has always shown me respect, I who am the youngest wife of the compound."

Layo's mind raced. What she had suspected about being the youngest wife was true. Bisi's mama was so unhappy, she had been driven to hurt Mama. Though Layo had suspected this unhappiness, she was shocked.

Bisi's mama sat down hard then, still shaking. The woman next to her touched Bisi's mama and called out that she was burning with fever. There was a flurry of activity as someone took Bisi. They called for the *babalawo,* and helping hands carried her off to Ogunsanwo compound.

The deep voice of the divinity called from behind the screen, "Obalufon."

The father of Obalara stood up from the bench he shared with other chiefs, then prostrated himself before the *oba.*

"What do you have to say for yourself? Remember that we can impose an ordeal to get at the truth. That woman claimed you had her make the clay core for a sacred object. Is that true?"

"Yes, Father."

"She may die from the power of the object."

"I thought that since she would not work with the finished product, she would be safe."

"Ah. We shall see. This illness shall be this

woman's punishment," the *oba* declared. "If she lives, she shall go free, and so shall you." The *oba* pronounced his judgment. "But if she dies, then you are banished from this city forever."

And the two drummers beat out the ending song.

Chapter 12

BISI'S MAMA HAD *IBA*. She had survived the first bout of fever. The father of Obalara had sent his *babalawo* to ensure her care. He also sent women from his household to aid the women of Ogunsanwo compound in nursing duties. Olade's mama turned all but one of them away, saying Ogunsanwo compound could take care of its own.

The father of Obalara's first wife was allowed to stay to supervise the women. Mama said, "We want them to know everything is being done to help Bisi's mama live. By allowing this woman control, we cannot be accused of sabotaging the father of Obalara."

Olade's mama had insisted that her *babalawo* see Bisi's mama, too. Old Mama had not had another bout of fever, and she was sure of her physician's abilities.

Layo and her mama sat on the veranda outside Mama's room, taking care of Bisi. The little boy was cranky. He clung to the veranda post and bounced up and down on his legs. He babbled, "*Iya, iya.*"

"Mama," Layo asked, "are you angry with me?"

"Yes, I am," Mama answered coolly. "You are a child, and you tried to take matters into your own hands with the father of Obalara. Your elders take care of you, and you must obey. Do you understand?"

"Yes, Mama," Layo said sadly. She loved her grandmother, and she didn't want the woman to be angry with her.

"And Layo," said Olade's mama, warming to the topic, "I know when I'm being insulted. I told you at the time the father of Obalara's statement about his work being better was no insult. You should have listened."

"Yes, Mama."

Mama began speaking quietly, as if to herself. "Perhaps you could marry Balogun. He is a titled elder and he has several wives already. The women there work clay."

Layo didn't want to think about *that* at all. To change her mama's thoughts, she asked, "Mama, are you very angry with Bisi's mama?"

"Well, that's a good question, child." She took Bisi and held him when he started to scream. "I might have been, but with this illness, I dare not say anything against her. I don't want to hurt her with my words." Mama sighed. "I feel bad, too. I have been thinking back to the time in Abiri when I wanted her to come with me. She was right. I let her know I wanted her help, and I just assumed she wanted to help me. I never asked. I did think she would say no if she really didn't want to come."

Toyin walked up. "I'll take Bisi and buy him a beancake," she said somberly, with a bow to Olade's mama.

"Thank you, Toyin," the woman answered, handing over the child.

Grandmother and granddaughter sat quietly, each with her own thoughts.

Things had been happening so quickly that Layo hadn't had the chance to consider her own fate. The *babalawo* had said she would get what she wanted. Just open the gate. She had wanted to help her grandmother and to learn about terra-cottas from her. She had begun that.

She had wanted to please her family. She had pleased Mama when she kept quiet about her ability.

She had wanted to give Bisi's mama a gift with her fine pot, and this she had done. But she hadn't thought about the consequences of marking her pot with Bisi's mama's mark. She couldn't have foreseen the events that had taken place, but she might have known the pot could have caused the woman some embarrassment.

She had wanted to find a flaw in Dada to avenge an insult. But those actions had made her look bad, not Dada.

120

Now Mama was angry with her. She had ruined her chances with Dada. She had slammed the gate shut on the man who had been the perfect choice for her.

Layo felt overwhelmed. This business of fate was confusing. She would get what she wanted, but how would she know what to choose? She was ashamed when the answer came to her. She had shut the gate on the wisdom of her grandmother.

Now was the time to acknowledge her grandmother's rightful power. Now she would open the gate to her knowledge and desires.

"Mama, I am sorry." She got up and bowed to her. "I will marry whomever you can find for me."

Mama did not have a chance to answer. Dada entered the compound gate.

He carried something wrapped in cloth, and he walked directly toward them. The young man prostrated himself at Mama's feet.

"Greeting to your house, Mother," he said.

"It will hear your greeting. Get up, Dada. It is good to see you."

Layo bowed to him when he got up.

"I have brought something to show you," he said to Layo.

Layo watched in surprise as he took an arm bracelet from the cloth.

"Oh, it's beautiful," she said. "May I touch it?"

She held in her hands a bracelet like no other

she had ever seen. Her titled elders wore arm bracelets of wood, or ivory, or iron, but this one was made of some other material. The material was heavy like iron, but it was brown-gold, not black. Little chameleons chased each other around the circle. Their features glowed in soft detail.

"Oh, it's so beautiful," she said again. "What is it made of?"

"This is bronze."

"Oh." Layo bowed deeply before her grandmother. "Thank you, Elder," she said to Dada, "now I truly understand."

"You can thank me in another way," he said.

"Yes, anything," Layo said. Joy at his presence stirred in her.

"If the father of Obalara leaves this city, I will go with him. He will take many followers to found a new city in the forest.

"There will be a lot of hard work, but many people will come when they hear about our wonderful village. It will soon become a city. And the founders will be the leaders, the chiefs.

"I will need a wife who is serious-minded, loyal, and high-spirited. May I go knowing that you are my betrothed?"

Every part of Layo cried *yes*. But she looked to her grandmother. "Mama?"

The old woman sighed. "Do you know, Dada, that there are people already in the forest? People who are not Yoruba. They have lived in their little villages since before time remembered. What will you do when you meet them?"

Layo waited for the answer as eagerly as her mama.

"Yes, I know there are forest people." He paused, then said, "Mama, I haven't before considered what will happen when we meet them. I suppose we will go around them until we get to the site where we want to have our city. If there are people already there, surely we will conquer them," he said firmly.

Layo's heart fell. To be a part of that.

"Layo," Mama said, "I wanted you to know."

Layo's voice caught as she held back tears. "Yes, Mama."

"Child, if it were not for this journey into the forest, would you *want* to marry Dada?"

"Oh yes, I want to marry this man." She bowed to Dada.

"You shall do that," she decided, "if the diviner gives his blessing."

Layo fulfilled her promise. She did not question the wisdom of her grandmother.

"My family will send members to your family, to do this properly. We can make arrangements for me to come to Abiri, to work for your family." He backed away, bowing.

Old Mama answered Layo's questioning eyes. "They will go whether you marry him or not. I cannot argue with them without my own status being exposed. Dada has all the qualities that make him the best choice for you. As for the people in the forest . . ."

"Yes, Mama," Layo interrupted. "Some will be like you. It is fate."

▲▲▲

"Bisi's mama will live," Mama told Layo days later. "The father of Obalara will stay here in Ife. He is powerful. This event will not damage *him* for long. Already the praise-singers make words from it that enhance his reputation."

"Then I will be a bride here in Ife?" The diviner had already approved the match.

"Yes."

Ah. Layo was so glad her marriage would not begin with the uprooting of the forest people.

"We will go to Abiri with Bisi's mama after her strength returns," Mama said. "Dada will come to the village at times to work for your parents, to fulfill his obligations to them. Then after your wedding, you will return here."

Layo missed her little village in the forest. And she was afraid of the eventual return to Ife.

Mama continued, "I have spoken with Bisi's mama, Layo. She regrets that she allowed ambition to rule her. Also, I am pleased that she spoke out to protect you at the *oba*'s court." Mama took Layo's hands in hers and spoke softly. "If the people in Abiri know of her actions, many years will pass before she can redeem herself. Life will be extraordinarily difficult for her. I have an idea. Perhaps we shouldn't tell them."

"Oh, Mama," Layo sang out. "I like that idea. One day I will be like Bisi's mama." She spoke of her fear. "I will be the youngest wife in my new compound. I like to think that the people there will be kind to me. Yes, Mama. But won't the people of Abiri eventually learn what happened?"

"Yes, but if we who are the injured parties deny it, can anyone argue?"

Layo nodded in agreement, contented.

She and her old mama went to work. Mama let her make a little child's pot. Layo slid her hands into the clay and dreamed of her life with Dada and the potters of his compound.

AFTERWORD

Did I go to Africa? That is the question people ask me when I tell them about my book.

No, I tell them. I did my traveling with books and museums and people. Using books in this case is ironic. The Yoruba did not have books. They were nonliterate. The diviner's verses, closely memorized, held much of the culture and history. Proverbs, legends, myths, and praise songs rounded out a person's education.

It is sad they were nonliterate, because of what the Yoruba people lost of their past during civil wars. The city of Ife was abandoned from 1850 to 1854, from 1878 to 1894, and probably other unknown dates through the centuries. For safekeeping, the people buried their religious relics, which were beautiful terra-cottas and bronzes with their own stories and meaning passed with spoken words through the generations. The people ran away to avoid being captured as slaves, and could not safely return for many years. The forest quickly grew up again and the mud houses collapsed. When the people did return, and they began to dig out mud for new homes, they found the bronzes and terra-cottas. Stories had been passed on, but no one knew which story and meaning went with which item. There was no written record saying, "Dig twelve paces from the old fig tree for the bronzes of the king."

So what did the Yoruba people do with the relics they dug up? Did they scratch their heads and put the objects on a shelf? Many items are in museums, but not all of them. That is the beautiful thing about Yoruba culture. They used the objects on their altars and in their dances. They gave the bronzes and terra-cottas new stories and new meanings to fit the day. They did not allow their culture to be frozen in a moment of time, a moment of loss.

When I dug up stories about the Yoruba, I had the same problem as those returning people. Many conflicting myths and legends were told. Which to use, which was right? I used the latest accepted information, but in the end, I imitated the Yoruba. I chose what worked to create a new story.

Which parts of this book come from the oral body of works which have finally been recorded, and which did I make up?

The Ifa verses in Chapter Four are from Wande Abimbola's book *Ifa Divination Poetry*. The proverb "The water that one is destined to drink does not flow past one" comes from *A Ki i:*

Yoruba Proscriptive and Prescriptive Proverbs by Oyekan Owomoyela.

Yoruba legend says Obalufon was a real person. He lived nearly a thousand years ago in the city of Ife, where he began the art of bronze casting. For that, he was deified, and stories have been told ever since to honor him.

Layo and her family are made-up people. The structure of the family is real though, and Layo's dilemmas of becoming the youngest wife of the compound and being held back in her talent until marriage are very real.

Now *you've* dug out this book. The Yoruba have existed as a culture for thousands of years. Despite terrible adversity, because of their positive outlook and their hope they are still going strong. We all can learn from that and, I hope, take knowledge from the past and create for ourselves new meaning.

About the Author

Janet E. Rupert began work on *The African Mask* after a course at Ohio State University aroused her interest in Nigeria and African history. She says, "When I discovered there was very little fiction for children about African culture, I was amazed and felt driven to help fill that void." In her research for this book, she had the guidance of a Yoruba anthropologist, Dr. Ojo Arewa.

Ms. Rupert was born in Ohio and now lives in Columbus, but she has also lived in a lighthouse on an island in Lake Erie. She and her husband and two children share their home with their cat, Merlin. *The African Mask* is her first book.